Ian McEwan

麦克尤恩 双语作品

当我们谈论科学时，我们在谈论什么
Science

〔英〕伊恩·麦克尤恩——著
孙灿——译

上海译文出版社

目 录

1. 文学、科学与人性   1
2. 物种独创性   30
3. 平行的传统   50
4. 世界末日蓝调   62
5. 自我   92

1

文学、科学与人性

对我们多数人而言,文学的伟大比科学的伟大更容易理解和接受。我们对什么才是伟大的小说家都各有想法,不管这想法是自己的,还是别人强加给我们的。无论是出于敬畏之情,还是出于乐趣、责任或是怀疑,只要一读《安娜·卡列尼娜》或是《包法利夫人》,我们就能立刻领会人们所说的伟大是什么意思。我们有无需中介便可与之直接产生联系的特权。从第一句起,我们便进入了某种灵异状态,能亲眼看见某个特定心灵的品质。只消几分钟,我们便可读完一个久被遗忘的下午的劳动成果,来自150年前那个独自工作的下午。那个曾被吐露的个人秘密,如今是我们的了。想象中的人物出现在我们面前,他们所处的历史和家庭环境都各具特色,个性也是如此。而我们,则见证和评判着将他们召唤出来的法术。

根据某种不言而喻的约定、某种作者和读者之间的合同,可以假定无论这些人有多么奇怪,我们都能轻而易举地理解他们,乃至欣赏他们的奇怪之处。为此,我们必须引入自己对于身而为人的常规理解。用认知心理学的话来说,我们有一套心智理论,多少可以自动理解身为他人的感受。倘若没有这种理解,根据精神病理学显示,我们事实上是无法形成和维持人际关系的,也无法理解表情或意图,或感知他人会如何理解我们自己。对于小说中展现给我们的特定例子,我们也带入了这种深切且广泛的理解。当索尔·贝娄笔下的赫索格①如小说角色常容易做的那样站在镜前时,他只戴着一顶新买的草帽,穿着短裤。他的母亲

> 希望他成为一位拉比②,而他现在却身穿短裤、头戴草帽,满脸都是深重的悲哀,带着本可以被宗

---

① 赫索格是美国作家索尔·贝娄的长篇小说作品《赫索格》的主人公,为20世纪60年代典型的美国犹太知识分子。他困惑于荒诞的现实,陷入了精神危机之中,但始终没有放弃对人类自身价值和人生意义的追求。

② 拉比(Rabbi)是犹太人中的特别阶层,是老师也是智者的象征,指接受过正规犹太教育,系统学习过《塔纳赫》《塔木德》等犹太教经典,担任犹太人社团或犹太教教会精神领袖或在犹太经学院中传授犹太教教义者,主要为有学问的学者。

教生活净化的愚蠢、完全的渴望,在他自己看来,和拉比面目迥异到了可怕的地步。那张嘴!——满载着欲望和难解的愤怒,笔挺的鼻梁时而显得无情,那双阴郁的眼睛!还有他的体型!——双臂和垂下的双手上,长长的青筋蜿蜒,这个古老的系统,比犹太人本身还要更为古远……光着双腿的他,看起来就像个印度教徒。

读者也许无法发自内心地理解赫索格的每种具体情况——身处20世纪中期的美国人、犹太人、城市居民、离异男子、被疏离的知识分子,而且可能年轻读者也不会对人近中年的懊悔产生同情,但逐步走向清算的自我审查有一种通用货币,从而提出了一种可笑、假天真的看法,认为一个人的生理机能——循环系统——比一个人的宗教出现得更早,因此也就暗示着它更能体现身为人类的本质。文学在作者与读者之间这种不言而喻的约定渠道中繁荣,提供了一幅心理地图,南北分指具体和一般。在最佳状态下,文学是普适的,恰好可以在最为地方性和具体化的点上精确地阐明人性。

科学的伟大对我们多数人来说更难领会。我们能列出一串据说很伟大的科学家名单,但很少有人有过那种能阐明成就特质的亲密接触。一部分原因是作品本身——它不邀请我们进去——它是客观化的,因此有距离感,被困难或看似无关的细节所侵蚀。数学也是一个障碍。此外,科学思想还快乐地游离于它们的创造者之外。科学家也许知道经典的运动定律,却从未读过牛顿在这方面的著作;或是从教科书里掌握了相对论,却没有读过爱因斯坦的狭义或广义相对论原文;又或是了解DNA的结构,却不必——或无需——直接读过克里克与沃森1953年的那篇论文①。

这是个罕见的恰当例子。他们的论文仅有1 200字,刊发在《自然》杂志上,结尾处是那个谦逊得出了名的结论:"我们并非没有注意到,我们假设的特定配对立刻显示出遗传物质可能有的复制机制。""我们并非没有注意到……":客厅礼节般的双重否定,却动人地坦率。它大致可以翻译为:"快看呐!我们找到了地球生命复制的机制,我们激动得要死,一分钟也睡不着。""我们并非没有注意到",就是我说的那种密切接触。在科学论文中直接遇到它,可不是常事。

然而就这一点来说,有一位杰出的科学家却几乎和小说家一样平易近人。不是科学家的人也完全可以理解,在达尔文的作品中,是什么成就了他的独特和伟大。一部分是因为,一系列良性的偶发事件让他走上了自己的

---

① 指《核酸的分子结构——DNA的结构》(*Molecular Structure of Nucleic Acids: A Structure for Deoxyribose Nucleic Acid*) 一文。

道路，积跬步终至千里。还有一部分是因为课题本身。自然史，或广义上的19世纪生物学，是一门描述性科学。物竞天择理论从本质上来说并不难理解，尽管它的内涵深远，用途强大，而且在科学方面产生的后果相当复杂——就像已故的比尔·汉密尔顿的计算生物学展现的那样。再有一部分是因为，达尔文尽管不是19世纪最好的散文家，但却特别健谈，情感丰富，亲密而坦诚。他写了很多信，还有许多本笔记。

让我们把他的人生当作小说来读，就像《赫索格》一样，朝着"大清算"一路进发。16岁的查尔斯正就读于爱丁堡大学，开始流露出对于医学研究的幻灭感。他给姐姐们写信说"我要去学做鸟类标本了，跟一个黑人学"。查尔斯跟一名解放了的奴隶约翰·爱德蒙斯顿学习动物标本剥制术，发觉自己的老师"很讨人喜欢，也很聪明"。爱德蒙斯顿向年轻的达尔文讲述了自己当奴隶的经历，还描述了热带雨林的奇观。达尔文一生都痛恨奴隶制度，并且，这种早年的交往也许和一本相对被忽视了的达尔文著作有些关系，而这本书正是我想讨论的。接下来的一年中，达尔文接触到了拉马克的进化思想，也在爱丁堡辩论社里听到了为科学唯物主义所作的激昂的无神论辩论。他成日沿着福斯湾海岸寻找海洋生物，在1827年的一本笔记中记录了对两种海洋无脊椎生物的详细观察。

因为查尔斯对以后从医并无兴趣,他父亲"建议我应该去当牧师。他对于我要成天野在外面表示了相当激烈的反对,但那似乎很可能就是我的目标"。所以,在18岁就读于剑桥大学的时候,他对自然史的喜好变成了酷爱。"我们该有多开心啊,"他给表哥写信说,"我们会捉到多棒的甲虫啊,要是我们能一块儿再去几个咱们的老地方,那该多好……我们可以定期在沼泽里搞活动。上帝保佑甲虫。"另一封信又写道:"我快闷死了,因为找不到人谈论昆虫。"到了最后两个学期,他的导师、植物学教授亨斯洛劝他去学地质学。

从剑桥毕业之后,他接到了亨斯洛转交的邀请,作为自然学家和船长的同伴登上"小猎犬号",前往南美洲开展政府调研。我们可以看到,在约西亚·韦奇伍德叔叔的帮助下,他为劝说父亲做出了争辩。"我必须重申,"诚挚的查尔斯恳求道,"我不觉得,在这之后我再去过稳定的生活,有什么不合适。"经过了数周的延误,接着是两次失败的出发之后,他于1831年12月27日起航。晕船多日后,"小猎犬号"却由于检疫措施,无法在加那利群岛的拉帕尔玛岛靠岸。但查尔斯在船尾支了一张网,天气很好,他抓了"许多稀奇的动物,足够我在船舱里忙活的"。最终,他们在佛得角群岛的圣地亚哥岛登陆,年轻人欣喜若狂。"这个岛屿给了我如此多的指导和乐趣,"他给父亲写信道,"关于风景,说什么都没用——对没有走出过欧洲的人描述截然不同的热带风景，就像对盲人解释色彩一样，毫无裨益……我总盼着把自己喜欢的东西写下来……因此你必须原谅我的狂喜，和对那些狂喜拙劣的表达。"

他喜欢在自己狭小的船舱房间里工作，为岩石、植物和动物的样本画图和进行文字描述，并把它们保存起来，寄回英国给亨斯洛。这种热情并没有随着探险的继续而衰退，反而更添日益增长的科学信心。他在给亨斯洛的信中写道：

> 最有趣的是，我找到了两种色彩优雅的涡虫，居住在干燥林里！它们和蜗牛之间的假性关系，是我见过最不寻常的事情……一些海洋物种所具有的结构是如此绝妙，我简直不敢相信自己的眼睛……今天我出去了，回来的时候就像驾驶着诺亚方舟，满载着各种动物……我找到了一只非常古怪的蜗牛，还有五花八门的蜘蛛、甲虫、蛇、蝎子。最后，我还打到了一只重1英担[①]的豚鼠……

5年之后，达尔文返回英国，年仅27岁，却已是

---

① 1英担为50.802千克。

颇有声望的科学家了。因为在回来之前,他已经寄回了大量保存下来的样本,并且对它们进行了描述,而且他脑中有关地球和珊瑚礁形成的理论也逐步成型了。达尔文29岁时,从"小猎犬号"航行归来仅仅两年,距离他出版《物种起源》(On the Origin of Species)还有21年,便向一本口袋笔记本吐露了那个简单、美好的想法的第一缕蛛丝马迹,其中就包含着伟大的文学才会给人带来的兴奋和启发:"人类起源现在得到了证实……了解狒狒的人会比洛克①对形而上学做出更大的贡献。"

然而,想通过《物种起源》本身来了解达尔文的伟大之处,却并不是一条轻松的路。把它当作一本书、而不是一个理论来读,非专业读者会被其中浩如烟海的例子吓到——这是达尔文拖稿的成果——而且要注意的是,最常被引用的部分要到全书最后几段才会出现。

达尔文是那种将工作完全渗透进生活中的科学家。他对于唐恩花园中蚯蚓的研究人尽皆知。他参加乡村集市,向养马、养狗和养猪的人提问,还去乡村比赛中找寻获奖蔬菜的种植者。他一向是慈爱的父亲,在一本笔记中记录道:"1839年12月27日,我的第一个孩子降生了。他刚一展现出各种表情,我便开始记录……"早

---

① 约翰·洛克(1632—1704),英国思想家、哲学家、著述家,其思想对于后代政治哲学发展产生巨大影响,被视为启蒙时代最具影响力的思想家和自由主义者。

在先天心智理论假设提出之前，达尔文就拿他的长子威廉做了实验，并得出了自己的结论：

> （威廉）6个月大几天的时候，他的保姆假装哭了，我看到他脸上立刻露出悲伤的表情，嘴角往下撇得很厉害。因此，我觉得一定是某种先天的情感告诉了他，保姆假装的哭泣表示忧伤，并且通过同情的本能，激发了他的忧伤。

骑马出行的时候，他停下来和一个女人说话，注意到她抬头看着背朝太阳的自己时，双眉是皱起来的。回家以后，他把自己的三个孩子带到屋外的花园里，让他们抬头看着天空明亮的部分。原因何在？"通过反射动作，三个人的轮匝肌、皱眉肌和锥状肌都有力地收缩……"

多年来，达尔文在忙于其他工作的同时，也在为《人类和动物的表情》（*The Expression of the Emotions in Man and Animals*）一书进行研究。这是他最为非凡和易懂的著作，充满了观察得来的细节和绝妙的推测，插图精美——这是最早使用照片的科学著作之一，还包括了一些他自己孩子噘嘴和大笑的照片——现在已经出到了第三版，由杰出的美国情感心理学家保罗·艾克曼编制并注释。达尔文不仅着手描述了狗、猫和人类的表情——我们在愤怒时眼周肌肉如何收缩,露出我们的犬齿,以及用艾克曼的话来说,我们是如何想用脸去触摸我们所爱的人——他还提出了一个难题:为什么?为什么我们难堪的时候脸会发红,而不是发白?为什么我们难过的时候,只有眉头会往上抬,而不是整条眉毛?为什么猫表达爱意的时候,会弓起脊背?他认为,一种情感就是一个生理状态,是心理变化的直接表现。在探究这些问题时,有许多有趣的"跑偏"和观察:台球运动员,尤其是新手,是如何试图用头部、乃至整个身体的运动来引导球打向目标的。一个坐在父母膝头生气的小孩,是如何抬起一边肩膀,往后一顶,表示拒绝的。在进行精细或困难的操作时,嘴巴是紧闭的。

在大量的细节背后,是更为基础的问题。是我们在高兴的时候学会了微笑,还是天生就会微笑?换言之,表情是所有文化和种族通用的,还是每种文化特有的?他给偏居大英帝国一隅的人们写信,请他们观察土著居民的表情。在英格兰,他把各种表情的照片给人们看,请大家做出评论。他也会借鉴自己的经验。这本书充满了逸闻趣事,没有科学腔,而且极具洞察力。达尔文认为,表情是进化的产物,因此具有普适性。他反对解剖学家查尔斯·贝尔爵士具有影响力的观点,后者认为,上帝在人类脸上创造了某些特定的肌肉,让他们能够彼此交流露感情，这些肌肉是动物界所没有的。在一则脚注中，艾克曼引用了贝尔书中的话："人类面部最了不起的肌肉是皱眉肌，它以某种无法解释的神秘作用联结着眉毛，却又不可抗拒地传达着心灵的想法。"达尔文也有贝尔这本书，他在这段话下面划了线，写道："我怀疑他从来没有解剖过猴子。"当然，这些肌肉正如达尔文展示的那样，也存在于其他灵长类动物身上。

通过展示控制表情的原理对灵长类动物和人类同样适用，达尔文论证了物种的连续性和渐变性——这对于他的进化论和驳斥基督教关于人类是特别的创造、有别于其他所有动物的观点，都有着普遍的重要意义。他还决心要通过普适性来证明，所有人种都是共同血统的后裔。在这一点上，他极力反对像阿加西这样的科学家所持的种族主义观点。这些科学家认为，非洲人次于欧洲人，因为他们是另一种劣等血统的后裔。在给胡克①的一封信中，达尔文提到，阿加西坚称"多物种"（指人）学说，"我敢说，八成是为了安慰蓄奴的南方人"。

现代古生物学及分子生物学表明达尔文是对的，而阿加西是错的：从解剖学上来说，我们都是同一批现代人类的后裔，他们或许 20 万年前才刚从非洲东部移居

---

① 约瑟夫·胡克（1817—1911），英国植物学家、探险家，地理植物学的开创者，达尔文的挚友。

到世界各地。各地气候的差异造成了人种的变化，但在很多情况下，真的只是肤表之差。我们盲目沉迷于这些差异，为征服和镇压寻找借口。正如达尔文所说：

> 人类展现出来的所有主要表情在全世界都是一样的。这一有趣的事实，为支持多个种族均为单一母系血统的后裔提供了新的论据。在种族分化时期之前，这一血统在生理结构上就几乎完全是人类，而且很大程度上，在思想上也是如此。

我们应该搞清楚通用表情的含义。吃一只蜗牛或是一片车达奶酪，也许会在一种文化中引起愉悦，在另一种文化中引起厌恶。但不管厌恶的原因是什么，都有一种通用的表情。用达尔文的话来说就是："嘴部大张，上唇用力收缩，鼻翼打皱。"表情和生理机能是进化的产物。但情感当然也是由文化塑造的。我们控制情感的方法、对待情感的态度、描述情感的方式都是后天习得的，并且因文化而异。然而，在人们通常所持有的情感概念背后，蕴含着普遍的人性。而且直到不久之前，也就是在20世纪很长一段时间里，这都是一个饱受诟病的概念。在达尔文死后很长一段时间里，他的作品都不受欢迎。但舆论现在已经变了，艾克曼的上佳版本成了出版界的盛事，受到了热烈的欢迎。

现在应该清楚的是，我认为文学作品中表达出的对想象力和独创性的运用支持了达尔文的观点。那些距离我们年代久远，或者文化背景与我们迥然不同的文学作品，我们是无法阅读和欣赏的，除非我们和作者都有着某种同样的感情基础、某些深层次的假设。注释版本可以说明历史环境、地方风俗或语言，总是有帮助的，但对阅读来说，绝不是根本需要。我们之间的共同之处，就像我们所有的异域差异一样，不同寻常。

我一开始就提到，地方性和普遍性就像是文学的两极。人们可以将文学看作是我们文化和基因遗传的编码。基因和文化这两个要素，各自都有着相互塑造的作用，因为作为灵长类动物，我们是高度社会化的生物，而且随着时间的推移，我们的社会环境施加了强大的适应性压力。这种由 E.O. 威尔逊[①]等人阐述的基因-文化协同进化，消融了先天与后天的对立。如果有人读了关于一群倭黑猩猩——倭黑猩猩和黑猩猩才是我们的近亲，达尔文说的狒狒不是——系统性的非入侵式观察记录，就会发现，其中预演了 19 世纪英国小说所有主要的题材：结盟和散伙，个体崛起和他人陨落，阴谋的策划，复仇，

---

① 爱德华·奥斯本·威尔逊（1929— ），美国生物学家，社会生物学的主要开创者，长期致力于研究蚂蚁等群居性昆虫。

感恩，受伤的骄傲，成败不一的求爱，丧亲和哀悼。在共有同一个祖先之后，我们和倭黑猩猩已经分开了500万年——考虑到这来来去去终究都和性有关（我这里指的是倭黑猩猩和19世纪小说），这是很长的一段时间，在此期间，成功的社会策略逐渐影响了某些特定基因的分布，但并没有影响其他基因。

我们具有天性，它的价值观对我们来说是不证自明的，甚至到了视而不见的地步，但如果我们是白蚁的话，这种天性就会有所不同了，这就是E.O.威尔逊想要说明的观点。为此，他虚构了一只受过高等教育的"白蚁院长"，在毕业典礼上为自己的白蚁同胞们做了一场激动人心的演讲：

    我们的祖先巨白蚁，在第三纪后期的快速进化中达到了10公斤，大脑也变得更大，并学会了使用信息素书写。自那以后，蚁道主义完善了道德哲学。准确地表达道德行为的道义论规则，如今已经变成了可能。这些规则大多不证自明，举世通用。它们正是蚁道的精髓。它们包括：对黑暗的热爱，以及对长有腐生担子菌的土壤深处的热爱；蚁群之间充满战争和贸易的群落生活集中性；生理等级制度的神圣性；工蚁阶层个人繁殖的罪恶性；对生殖手足的谜之深爱,在它们交配的瞬间变成了仇恨;对个人权利之罪的排斥;对信息素之歌无穷无尽的审美愉悦感;蜕皮之后,从巢伴肛门进食的审美愉悦感,同类相残的快乐,以及生病或受伤时献出自己的身体以供同类食用的快乐……某些具有蚁道主义倾向的科学家,尤其是动物行为学家和社会生物学家,认为我们的社会组织是由我们的基因塑造的,因此我们的道德戒律仅仅反映了白蚁进化的特性。他们声称,道德哲学必须考虑白蚁大脑的结构和该物种的进化史。社会化是由基因引导的,有些形式的社会化几乎是不可避免的。这一提议引起了重大的学术争议……

这就是说,无论它是萨迦冒险故事、象形诗、成长教育小说还是俳句,并且不管它是什么时候写的、由哪个蚁群写的,只要读了一两行,你就会知道这是白蚁文学。由白蚁文学传统推断,我们可以说,我们自己的人类文学与其说是对人性的定义,不如说是对人性的例证。

如果有超越文化的人类共性,那么由此可见,它们不会改变,或不会轻易改变。如果在历史上我们确实发生了改变,那么根据定义,改变的并不是人性,而是在某种特定时间和环境下的某些特性。然而,也有一些作家喜欢这样表明自己的观点:他们假定人性本质脆弱,容易受到突发事件的影响——刺激的革命性进步，或是深感遗憾的退化，并将改变的时刻定义为始终不可抗拒的知识追求。我想在这件事的精确性上，还没有人可以超越弗吉尼亚·伍尔夫，尽管她确实对实际日期略带讽刺地模糊其词。"在1910年12月或前后，"她在随笔《小说人物》(*Character in Fiction*) 中写道，"人性改变了。"当然，伍尔夫眼中分隔她和父母两代人的巨大鸿沟先入为主，占据了她的思想。有一件著名的轶事真假难辨，但你会希望它是真的。那是1908年，里顿·斯特拉奇走进一间客厅，遇见了弗吉尼亚和她的姐姐。他指着瓦妮莎裙子上的一块污渍问道："精液？"弗吉尼亚写道："那一个词，让所有沉默和矜持的障碍都土崩瓦解。"19世纪正式结束。世界再也不一样了。

我记得，60年代和70年代早期也有过类似的末世言论。"人性永远改变了"，当时有过这样的宣言，在1967年伍德斯托克附近的一片田野里，或是同年伴随着《佩珀军士》(*Sergeant Pepper*) 的发行，又或是前一年，在旧金山某条不起眼的街道上。水瓶座时代①已经曙光微现，事情再也不一样了。

T.S. 艾略特在他的随笔《玄学派诗人》(*The Metaphysical Poets*) 中不像弗吉尼亚·伍尔夫那样令人

---

① 水瓶座时代指爱与和平的年代。

头晕目眩，但口吻也同样确定。他发现，在17世纪，"一种感性的分裂开始了，我们从未从中完全恢复过来"。他说的自然是英国诗人，他们"拥有一种感性机制，可以吞噬任何种类的经验"，但我想我们可以假定，他认为他们通常和其他人的生理特征一样。他的理论正如他承认的那样，也许过于草率，无法令人信服，既表达了艾略特的遗憾（这种分裂不是好事），也表达了他的希望（那些现代诗人将按照他的处方重新定义现代感性，从而可以扭转这种分裂）。

雅各布·布克哈特在《意大利文艺复兴时期的文化》（*The Civilization of the Renaissance in Italy*）一书中定义了他自己的选择时刻，觉察到了一种绽放，不仅在于人性，也在于意识本身，"在中世纪"，他写道：

> 人类意识的两面——向内和向外的——都在共同的面纱下躺着做梦，或半梦半醒。人类只有在作为种族、民族、党派、家庭或社团的一员时，才会对自我产生意识……但到了13世纪将尽的时候，意大利开始充满了个体性；对人类个性的禁令解除了。

法国历史学家菲利普·阿里埃斯定义了18世纪人类情感的一个根本转变，在那时，父母开始感受到对子女自觉的爱。在那之前，孩子只不过就是一个无能的小大人，容易被疾病夺去生命，因此不值得投入太多感情。上千座中世纪的墓碑，和上面悼念逝去孩子的感人碑文，也许埋葬了这一特定的理论，但阿里埃斯的作品说明，在对人性改变的决定性时刻的追求中，有一种次要的或是平行的野心——那就是，旨在定位我们现代性的根源。这或多或少是思想史的中心议题——询问在什么时刻、何种环境下，我们变得可以为自我所认知。至少有些候选项会是你熟悉的：一万年前农业的发明，或是与之紧密相关的——逐出伊甸园。又或是《哈姆雷特》的诞生，书中描写的那个男人是如此痛苦、无聊、优柔寡断，总是在活受罪，所以我们打心眼里接受了他，并且发现以前的文学作品里没有他这样的人。我们可以把现代思想的开端确定为17世纪的科学革命；将人口聚集在城市里，最终使大众消费、大众政党和大众传播成为可能的农业或工业革命；带来了最巧妙或故意的抽离感的卡夫卡的写作；或是刚刚发明了几千年的书写本身，它使文化传播的几何增长成为可能；爱因斯坦狭义相对论和广义相对论的发表，《春之祭》的首场演出，乔伊斯《尤利西斯》的出版，或是在广岛投下的核武器——在那之后我们接受了对整个星球的管理，无论我们是否情愿。有些人曾经选择攻占冬宫，但我却更喜欢华兹华斯早期朴实无华、充满了会话式反思的诗歌；或是与之相关的英国或法国启蒙运动，以及世界人权的发明。

从另一方面来说，生物学的观点很长，措辞也不华丽，尽管我觉得趣味性也不差：人们所说的并不是某个时刻，而是一段无法估量、不可复原的时间，只留下了一捧骨制和石制的史前器物，需要穷尽我们的天才来解读。随着大脑新皮层以每 10 万年增加一茶勺灰质的惊人速度进化，原始人类制造出了工具，学会了语言，意识到了自己和他人的存在，也意识到了自己必死的命运，有了来生的看法，因此会埋葬死者。3 万年前灭绝的尼安德特人可能是最先进入现代的。但他们还是不够现代化，无法在这种节奏中生存下去。

你可以说，所有这些描述中所追求的，都相当于世俗的创世神话。文学作家们似乎更喜欢爆炸性的决定性时刻，奇迹的诞生，而不是无趣的连续性极小变化。整个文化时间跨度或多或少都可以包含其中，当我们询问：谁是最古老的？谁是现代人类乌尔人？——是线粒体夏娃，还是艾伦·图灵[①]？

我们对现代性根源感兴趣，不仅仅是社会加速变革的结果：在与过去决裂的决定性时刻这一理念中蕴含着一种概念，那就是人性是特定历史的产物，由共同的

[①] 艾伦·图灵（1912—1954），英国数学家、逻辑学家，被视为"计算机之父"。

价值观和某种特定文明中的抚养环境所塑造——换句话说，除了在特定时间和特定文化中发展出来之外，根本就没有人性。按照这一观点，大脑就像是一台万能的、具有无限适应性的计算机，根据少量固定规则在运行。我们生来就像一张白板，是我们的时代塑造了我们。

这种观点，有人称之为标准社会科学模型，也有人称之为环境决定论，在20世纪占据了主导地位，尤其是在上半叶。它扎根于人类学，尤其是在玛格丽特·米德①及其追随者的著作中，也植根于行为心理学。米德在发表于1935年的《三个原始部落的性别与气质》(*Sex and Temperament in Three Primitive Societies*) 中写道："我们不得不做出这样的结论：人性几乎具有难以置信的可塑性，可以根据对比鲜明的文化条件做出精确而截然不同的反应。"这一观点在社会科学界得到了广泛的认可，并且在战后数年间固化为一种带有清晰政治维度的教条。要是从现存的生物层面来挑战它，曾一度会沦为学术界、乃至社会上的贱民。和基督教神学家一样，文化相对主义者将我们从所有生物学的限制中解放出来，并且把人类和地球上其他一切生物区分开来。有了这一观点，受过教育的男女宣布在某个特定日期人性会发生

---

① 玛格丽特·米德（1901—1978），美国人类学家，美国现代人类学形成过程中最重要的学者之一。

转变时，就有了坚实的认识论基础——世界塑造了我们，因此当世界发生剧变时，我们的本质也会发生剧变。这一切都可能发生，如同弗吉尼亚·伍尔夫自己观察到的那样，"在1910年12月或前后"。

1928年，著名行为学家、约翰·霍普金斯大学心理学教授约翰·华生出版了一本具有影响力的育儿著作。正如克里斯蒂娜·哈德门特在她了不起的作品《梦想宝贝》(*Dream Babies*)中展示的那样，要想了解一个社会的集体意识和它对人性的看法，几乎没有比它出品的育儿手册更好的窗口了。华生写道：

> 给我一打健康的、身体结构良好的婴儿，再给我一个特定的环境来把他们养大，我保证可以任选一个，把他训练成我可能会选择的任意一种专业人士——医生、律师、大商人，哦对，甚至是乞丐和小偷，不管他的天赋、嗜好、倾向、能力和他祖先的职业与种族如何。

在他手中，人性犹如黏土一般。我不禁觉得，以下出自华生育儿著作《婴幼儿心理护理》(*The Psychological Care of Young Infants*)的段落，除了它无意造成的喜剧效果之外，还反映或预示了一个世纪以来，在人性塑造方面注定失败的悲剧性社会实验，并且向我们展示了一种扭曲而缺乏证据的科学，和歪曲达尔文的著作来宣扬种族优越论的伪科学一样荒诞不经：

> 抚养孩子的明智之举是把他们当作年轻的成年人来对待。小心而慎重地为他们穿衣和洗澡。你自己的行为举止永远要客观、温和而坚定。绝不要拥抱和亲吻他们。绝不要让他们坐在你的大腿上。如果一定要的话，在他们道晚安的时候亲吻一次他们的额头。和他们握手道早安。当他们出色地完成了一件困难的任务时，轻拍他们的头……多数时间把孩子放在屋外的后院里……孩子一生下来就这么做……让孩子几乎从出生那一刻起，就学着自己克服困难……远离你关切的目光。如果你的心太软，一定要看着孩子，那就挖一个窥视孔，这样你看的时候不会被孩子发现，或是用潜望镜。

华生的书在当时取得了巨大的成功，《大西洋月刊》称其为"上天赐给父母的恩物"。

持有这些观点的米德和华生，只是众多宣扬人性具有近乎无限可塑性的人物中突出的两位。他们的观点在民众和大学中获得了广泛的支持，后继者今天仍以各种形式蓬勃发展。没有人应该怀疑，标准模式背后隐藏着一些良好的动机。尤其是玛格丽特·米德，在她从事研究的时代，欧洲帝国已经进行了合并，却尚未开始分崩离析，她的著作中有着强烈的反种族主义元素，并且她坚决反对原始劣等性的倨傲观点，坚持每一种文化都必须以它自己的方式来评判。在米德和华生最为活跃的时候，人类依然对苏联革命抱有巨大的希望。如果学习成就了现在的我们，那么只要我们享有同样的环境，就可以消除不平等。教给父母合适的育儿方法，就会出现改良版的新一代。社会政策的制定者可以从根本上重塑人性。我们可以变得完美，可以通过彻底改变社会环境来纠正过去的错误和不平等。社会达尔文主义和优生学的残酷与荒谬，以及后来希特勒时期的德国社会政策带来的新的威胁，都引发了人们对生物学视角的厌恶，从而帮助人们确立了一种信念：天性可以由社会塑造，通过对天性的设计，大家都会变得更好。

事实上，在二战之后的数十年间，自由的科学探索都长期笼罩在第三帝国的阴影之下。心理学的众多分支都被知识的恐惧所禁锢，受制于不久前的历史，不再把大脑看作是具有适应性力量的生物学产物。尽管在此期间，相邻的生物学系自20世纪40年代以来，由达尔文学说联合孟德尔遗传学和分子生物学，形成了强大的联盟，被称为"现代综合进化论"。

50年代后期，年轻的保罗·艾克曼出发前往新几内亚。他还没有什么属于自己的坚定看法，只带着一些大头照和半身照，上面是现代美国人，做着各种表情——惊讶、恐惧、厌恶、喜悦等等。他的样本群是源自石器时代的高地人，以前没有或是几乎没有接触过现代世界。但他发现，他们可以为每种表情编出一眼就能看出来的故事。他们还为他模仿出了面部表情，以回应他给他们讲的故事——"你遇到一头死了好几天的猪"。他的研究，以及后来以日本人和美国人为对象的实验——该实验设计巧妙，考虑到了不同文化的表达规则——都清楚地证明达尔文的结论是正确的。正如艾克曼所写：

> 社会经验会影响对待情感的态度，创造出表达和感受的规则，开发和调整最能迅速唤起某种情感的特定场合。然而，我们情感的*表现*，肌肉运动的特定结构，似乎是固定的，使得不同时代、不同文化的人可以相互理解，也使得同种文化中，无论是陌生人还是亲密的朋友，都能互相理解。

去新几内亚之前，他拜访了玛格丽特·米德。她坚定地认为，各个文化之间的面部表情各不相同，就像风俗和价值观一样。她对艾克曼的研究显然无动于衷。然而到了晚年,她却在1972年的自传中解释说,她和同事之所以不愿意考虑行为的生物学基础,是因为担心会带来政治后果。多么奇怪啊,这种历史环境的反转——对米德来说,表情或人性中的普遍性似乎会为种族主义提供支持,但对达尔文来说,这些考虑则破坏了种族主义不堪一击的理论基础。

米德和她那一代的人类学家,带着笔记本、礼物和体面的目的来到了石器时代定居点。在与受试者互致微笑和问候时,他们还不完全理解(尽管达尔文和大多数的小说家应该可以告诉他们),想要从事自己的研究,需要多么大量的共有人性和共有假设,而且自己也已经在利用这些人性和假设了。随着最后这些珍贵文化的消失,人们又重新审视了数据。唐纳德·布朗在他的《人类共性》(*Human Universals*,1991)一书中,编写了一份人类个体和社会的共性列表。列表很长,考虑到所有可能的行为模式范围几乎是无限的,因此也很具体。读它的时候,有必要把威尔逊的白蚁院长记在心里。布朗囊括了——我任选几个吧——工具制造,占压倒性多数的右撇子,特定的童年恐惧,认识到他人拥有内心生活,交易,赠予礼物,正义观念,八卦的重要性,好客,阶层等等。布朗描述了他所谓的"普世者"(Universal People),他们融合了人类全部共同拥有的特征,有趣的是,他花了大量的篇幅专讲语言——依然非常具体。比如说，普世者的语言有元音之间的对比，也有停顿和非停顿之间的对比。他们的语言具有象征性，总是包含名词、动词和所有格。对语言运用得特别熟练，一定会带来威望。在更高层次的精神功能上，这无疑是人类家庭的纽带。我们现在知道，没有任何一台磁盘空白的全能机器可以像儿童那样快速、灵巧地学习语言。一个3岁的孩子每天都要解决大量的不恰当问题。语言天分是我们天性的核心。

在我们拥挤的星球上，我们已经无法再拜访未曾被摩登时代所染指的石器时代居民了。米德和她同时代的人绝对不会想要提出这个问题：我们和这些人之间到底有什么相同点？人类学家也不会再有首次接触的机会了。但我们可以把手伸向书架。文学一定就是我们的人类学。下面这段描写——来自2 700年之前——说的是一个女人等她心爱的丈夫回家，等了20多年。有人告诉她，他终于回来了，就在楼下，她必须去迎接他。但，她问自己，那真的是他吗？

> 她走下楼上的睡房，心中左思右想……
> 是离着心爱的丈夫，开口发问？
> 还是走上前去，握住他的手，亲吻他的头颅？
> 她跨过石凿的门槛，步入厅中，

> 就着亮光落坐,面对奥德修斯,贴着对面的墙壁。
> 而他则坐在高耸的房柱旁,眼睛看着地面,
> 静等雍贵的妻子,有何话语要说,眼见他在身旁。
> 她静坐良久,默不作声……心中惊奇诧异,
> 不时注目观望,盯着他的脸面。
> 一瞬间他似乎……就是丈夫奥德修斯,
> 活生生在眼前——
> 下一瞬间,不,他不是她认识的丈夫,
> 她眼前只有一堆破衣烂衫。①

所以,尚不确定的裴奈罗珮告诉奥德修斯,他们要分房睡,她还下令将婚床搬出卧室。但他当然知道,这张床是搬不动的——床是他自己钉起来的,他还提醒了她,他是怎么做这张床的。从而他毫无疑问地证实了,自己真的是她的丈夫。但他现在不开心了,因为她觉得自己是冒牌货,他们两口子要吵架了。

> 裴奈罗珮双膝发软,心力酥散,
> 她已听知确切的话证,从奥德修斯的言谈,

---

① 译文节选自《荷马史诗:伊利亚特·奥德赛》(上海译文出版社,2016)。

顿时热泪盈眶，冲跑着奔扑上前，

展开双臂，抱住奥德修斯的脖圈，亲吻他的头颅，说道：

"不要生我的气，奥德修斯，凡人中你是最通情达理的一员！

神明给我们悲难，心生嫉烦，

不愿看着我俩总在一起，共享我们的青春，双双迈过暮年的门槛。

所以，不要生气，不要把我责备，

只因我，在首次见你之际，不曾像现在这样，吻迎你的归来……

我的心里总在担惊受怕，害怕有人会出现在我面前，花言巧语，将我欺骗。"[①]

习俗也许不同了——可能走廊里躺着死去的求婚者，却不会有杀人指控——但我们在这几行诗中认出了人类的本质。我们在情感和表达方面依然故我。正如达尔文在《表情》一书的结论中所说："情感的语言……必然对人类的福祉具有重要性。"在荷马的例子中，我们扩展了艾克曼的"跨代理解"——至少跨越了130代。

---

① 译文节选自《荷马史诗：伊利亚特·奥德赛》（上海译文出版社，2016）。

人类基因组测序组织（The Human Genome Sequencing Consortium）在2001年《自然》杂志上发布了报告，结尾是这么写的："最终，我们并非没有注意到，我们对人类基因组了解得越多，有待探索的也就越多。"这种与传统相呼应的致敬方式，势必会吸引喜爱文学现代主义的那些人。随着人类基因组测序的完成，我们有理由发问，这到底是谁的基因组？哪一位幸运儿被选中代表我们所有人？谁是"普世之人"？答案是，15个人的基因被融合在一起，组成了一个小说家也许会虚构出来的那种合成的、貌似真实的、想象的人，因此我们此刻注视着的，是一个带有隐喻色彩的聚合体，来自两种对我们的状况伟大而迥异的调查形式——文学和科学。把我们、我们共同的天性联系在一起的东西，就是文学向来刻意而又无奈地想要表达的。而这种普遍性，也正是迈入又一振奋人心阶段的生物科学要进一步探索的。

希拉里讲座，牛津，2003。

2

物种独创性

1858年6月,一个细长的包裹,从荷属东印度群岛德那第寄到了查尔斯·达尔文位于肯特郡唐恩村的乡间别墅中。他或许已经认出,上面是阿尔弗雷德·华莱士[①]的笔迹。他和华莱士通过信,希望从他那里获得一些样本。但达尔文发现,包裹中是一封投稿信,还附着一篇小论文。而这篇论文,将会改变达尔文的人生。

在那个事关重大的早晨,华莱士这20页纸在它们的读者看来,似乎涵盖了自然选择进化论的所有主要思想。而那些思想正是达尔文研究了20多年,以为归他自己所独有的——并且他还没有将其发表。华莱士孤军奋战,没人鼓励他,也没有钱,凭借的是给收藏家寄送样本时积累的大量自然史经验。他简明扼要地表述了基本原理和信息来源,这些也都是达尔文所熟悉的:人为的选择,生存的斗争,竞争与灭绝,物种变化的方式——通过客观、可描述的过程,借助无须神明干预的逻辑,演变为不同的形态。华莱士和达尔文一样,也受到过查尔斯·莱尔地质学推测和托马斯·马尔萨斯人口理论的影响。

投稿信中,华莱士礼貌地请达尔文把论文转交给莱尔。眼下,达尔文本可以悄悄毁掉华莱士的包裹,而不走漏半点风声——包裹寄了好几个月才到,而且在19世纪中期,与荷属东印度群岛之间的邮政往来几乎一点也不可靠。但达尔文是正人君子,而且知道他永远都无法原谅自己做出这种下流勾当。可他也非常郁闷。达尔文当天就把华莱士的论文寄给了莱尔,还附上了一封自己的信,信中哀叹道:"故我所有的独创性,不管总计几何,都将被击个粉碎了。"他很惊讶,自己对拥有优先权和成为第一人的感情竟如此之深。正如珍妮特·布朗恩在她的《达尔文传》中指出的那样,他研究发现的兴奋已经被占有和所有权的深切焦虑所取代了。他被低落情绪——屈辱、恼怒、仇恨——偷袭了。用一句常被引用的话说,他"满心都是毫无价值的情感"。

---

① 阿尔弗雷德·华莱士(1823—1913),英国博物学家、探险家、地理学家、人类学家与生物学家。

他迟迟不发表自己的研究，是希望它尽善尽美，多积累些例子，尽可能让它免受反驳。当然，他也意识到了自己的研究对神学的影响——这也让他格外小心。但他已经被别人"占了先机"。所以那天他决定，必须把优先权拱手相让给华莱士。他必须，他写道："听天由命。"

不出一天，就有了更让他急着去担心的事情。他15岁的女儿汉丽埃塔病了，怕是得了白喉。第二天，他和艾玛的第十个孩子、也是最小的宝宝查尔斯发起了烧。与此同时，莱尔正在敦促达尔文不要让步，把"草稿"发表出来，这样就可以最终证明达尔文比华莱士有优先权。

达尔文和家人轮流照顾生病的宝宝，无法做出任何决定，只能将此事交由好友约瑟夫·胡克和莱尔处理。他们商议之后，提议将达尔文的"草稿"和华莱士的论文在林奈学会①的会议上一并宣读，将两篇文章都发表在学会的学术期刊上。速度很重要。华莱士也许已经把他的论文寄给了某家杂志，这样一来，达尔文抢占先机的希望就会落空，或至少要打个折扣。已经没时间征求华莱士的许可来宣读他的论文了。

然而，还没等达尔文考虑这一提议，宝宝就夭折

---

① 伦敦林奈学会是一个学术学会，致力于研究和传播关于自然史、进化论和生物分类学的信息，拥有一些重要的生物标本、手稿和文献收藏，并出版动植物生物学的学术期刊和书籍。此学会建立于1788年，得名于生物分类系统早期建立者、瑞典博物学家卡尔·冯·林奈。

了。悲痛的达尔文匆匆整理了一遍稿子，交由胡克编辑。1844年的那套笔记尽管已经过时了，但似乎成了确定优先权的最终依据，因为上面有胡克用铅笔写下的批注。在之后1857年达尔文给哈佛大学植物学教授阿萨·格雷的信中，他简要阐述了关于自然选择进化论的思想。

维多利亚时代的大都市科学界是个封闭的小圈子，莱尔、胡克和达尔文都是知名的圈内人士。华莱士则是圈外人。他的出身卑微得多，就算有人知道他，也只知道他是为绅士专家提供物料的。按照林奈学会的惯例，两篇做出同样贡献的文章，要按照作者姓名字母表顺序宣读。于是，在达尔文缺席的情况下——那天他和艾玛要为宝宝下葬——会议宣读了他1844年的笔记，接着是1857年那封详尽的信件，然后才几乎像是做脚注般，读了读华莱士1858年的论文。

达尔文钻研多年，要深入得多，当然应该拥有优先权。华莱士难以参透自然选择的蕴意，在之后的岁月里，也不愿承认人类也会受到进化变异的影响。但关键在于，达尔文为失去占有权而深感屈辱。正如他后来给胡克写信说："我总觉得很可能会被别人抢占先机，但我幻想自己心胸足够开阔，不会在意。"

胡克开始敦促他的朋友，写一篇关于自然选择的正式科学论文。达尔文反对。他要把所有的事实都列出来，一篇论文写不下。但胡克执意如此行事，于是达尔文便开始写了，假以时日，文章变成了《物种起源》一书。按照布朗恩的描述，"压抑多年的谨慎"突然释放。在唐恩的别墅中，达尔文没有用书桌，而是坐在一张扶手椅上，大腿上铺了一块木板，发了疯似的写着。"多年来所有的思考，"布朗恩写道，"在这几个月的最终洞察中达到了高潮……华莱士燃起了他内心的激情。"

《起源》一书耗时13个月写成，表现出了非凡的智力成就：洞见成熟，学养和观察力深厚，对事实进行了梳理，用近乎无可辩驳的论据阐明了对自然进程的深刻洞察。他本不想颠覆妻子艾玛的宗教信仰，也不想否定科学界同事对神学的确定，也不想担任希望渺茫的习俗破坏者角色，成为维多利亚社会的激进反对者——但这些不情不愿全都被抛到了脑后，因为他害怕另一个人会把他相信属于他自己的想法占为己有，并获得赞誉。

在现代，我们已经把至关重要和经久不衰的独创性观念视为艺术——文学、绘画与电影——中理所当然的事情了。尽管有各种理论上的反对意见，它仍然是我们质量观的核心。它承载着一种"新"的、以上帝的方式无中生有的理念。"完美的非借鉴感"，就像柯勒律治对华兹华斯诗歌的评价一样。独创性和强大的个体意识是不可分割的，而且这种个体性的界限也受到了强有力的保护。

在传统社会里，遵从某些受到尊崇的模式和惯例是一种规范。壶、雕刻和精美的编织不需要签名。相反，现代手工制品则带有个性的印记。作品即是签名。个人真正地拥有他或她自己的作品，享有对作品的权利，通过作品来定义自己。作品是私人财产，不可侵犯。围绕着这种所有权，已经形成了一套庞大的法律体系。那些没有签署《伯尔尼公约》①和其他知识产权相关的国际协议的国家，会发现自己被排除在全球化文化的主流之外。艺术家拥有自己的作品，瞪着眼睛坐在上面，就像孵蛋母鸡一样。每当剽窃丑闻爆发的时候，我们就会看到独创性和个体化融合后的剧烈反应。

护封上的照片，尽管与欣赏一本小说几乎毫无干系，却确定了所有权。这是我，它说，而且你手里的东西是我的。或者是我。我们也在围绕着艺术家的个人崇拜中看到了这一点——用个体化和个性去激发近乎宗教化的虔诚。格拉斯米尔②的大巴旅行团，海明威、毕加索或聂鲁达崇拜。这些都是大人物——他们的人生有时比他们的艺术更让我们着迷。

---

① 即《保护文学和艺术作品伯尔尼公约》，是关于著作权保护的国际条约，1886 年 9 月 9 日制定于瑞士伯尔尼。
② 英国诗人威廉·华兹华斯故居所在地。

这种着迷出现得相对较晚。莎士比亚、巴赫、莫扎特乃至贝多芬,在他们那个年代都没有受到过崇拜,他们的社会地位并不显赫,既不如他们的资助者,又不如拜伦或是肖邦,也不如今天的诺奖得主。谦逊的艺术家是如何荣升为俗世之神的,这是一个富有争议的重大话题,是对个体化和现代性长期探讨的一个分支。可能的原因列表是大家耳熟能详的——资本主义,增长的休闲阶层,新教信仰,浪漫主义运动,通讯新技术,工业革命后专利法的制定。其中的一些或是全部带我们走到了这一步:如今,对个体和她创造力的鉴别是彻底、自动和毫无疑问的。今天,在自己写的书上为读者签名的小说家,以及排队等待自己买的书被签名的读者,合伙密谋了这一场自我与艺术的联姻。

还有一种与之对立的艺术创作概念,尽管被艺术家、评论家和理论家以多种形式表达过,但却从未在学界以外生根。这种观点认为,当然没有人能够逃离历史。无中生有是不可能的,即使是天才,也会被环境的约束和机遇所限制。艺术家只不过是历史和文化用来演奏的乐器。不论艺术家的作品与传统相符或是相悖,他都只能无奈地成为传统的产物。奥登[①]散文的标题《染匠之手》

[①] 威斯坦·休·奥登(1907—1973),著作多署名 W. H. Auden,英裔美籍诗人,1968年获诺贝尔文学奖提名。

(*The Dyer's Hand*),无非是对这一含义温和的表达。前人开发的技巧和惯例——比如说透视法，或是自由间接文体（受人物主观状态影响的第三人称叙事），都是唾手可得的现成的工具，而且具有深远的影响。艺术首先是一种代代相传的对话。有意义的呼应、戏仿、引用、反叛、致敬和仿作都有它们的位置。文化,而非个人才华,才是支配力量；在创意写作课上，年轻的写作者被告知，如果他们阅读面不广，就更有可能无奈地被那些他们不了解其作品的作家所影响。

这种文化传承的观点，对科学天生友好。达尔文以各种进化论观点为背景开展研究，包括他祖父伊拉斯谟斯[①]的观点。达尔文依赖动物饲养者、鸽子迷、自然历史学家的观察，以及马尔萨斯和莱尔的研究。另一位伟大的创造者爱因斯坦，如果没有包括亨德里克·洛伦兹[②]和马克斯·普朗克[③]在内无数其他人的帮助，是不可能开始他的狭义相对论研究的。他完全依赖数学来表达自己的思想。（牛顿"站在巨人肩膀上"的名言几年前被反转了，

[①] 伊拉斯谟斯·达尔文（1731—1802），英国医学家、诗人、发明家、植物学家与生理学家。
[②] 亨德里克·洛伦兹（1853—1928），荷兰理论物理学家、数学家，经典电子论的创立者。
[③] 马克斯·普朗克（1858—1947），德国著名物理学家，量子力学的重要创始人之一，和爱因斯坦并称为20世纪最重要的两大物理学家。

借以说明前人在科学中的力量:"如果我没有别人看得远,那是因为巨人站在我的肩膀上。")

考虑到 20 世纪中期科学家们已有的工具,包括 X 射线晶体学,再考虑到流传的假设,以及已经在这一领域开始进行研究的不同群体,DNA 迟早会被张三或李四描述出来的。在纯理性和科学发展的领域中,谁先到达那里,应该都无所谓。如果那个人是莱纳斯·鲍林①,而不是克里克与沃森,又会给公共利益带来什么不同呢?但领先了几个月,却给克里克与沃森的人生带来了多少不同啊。

对造福全人类而言,不管发现氧气的是约瑟夫·普里斯特利②还是安托·拉瓦锡③,也不管发明微积分的是艾萨克·牛顿还是戈特弗里德·莱布尼茨④,又有什么关系呢?

再来看看另一个著名的"优先权焦虑"时刻。在这一时刻到来前的 10 年间,爱因斯坦都致力于一个雄心勃勃的计划,要将他 1905 年提出的狭义相对论"广义化"。随着他的思想在发表后数年间的不断发展,他预测出光

---

① 莱纳斯·鲍林(1901—1994),美国著名化学家,量子化学和结构生物学的先驱者之一。1954 年因在化学键方面的工作取得诺贝尔化学奖,1962 年因反对核弹在地面测试的行动获得诺贝尔和平奖。
② 约瑟夫·普里斯特利(1733—1804),英国化学家。
③ 安托·拉瓦锡(1743—1794),法国化学家、生物学家。
④ 戈特弗里德·莱布尼茨(1646—1716),德国哲学家、数学家。

会受到万有引力的影响。他的传记作家沃尔特·艾萨克森指出，爱因斯坦的成功到那时为止，都"建立在发现自然界潜在物理原理的特殊才能上"，而把提供最佳数学表达这种较为平凡的任务留给了别人。"然而，"艾萨克森指出，"到1912年，爱因斯坦开始意识到，数学可以成为发现——而不仅仅是描述——自然法则的工具。"

艾萨克森引用了物理学家詹姆斯·哈特尔的话："广义相对论的核心思想就是，万有引力源于时空弯曲。"它要描述两个互补的过程——物质如何被引力场影响，以及物质如何在时空中产生引力场，并使其弯曲。这些惊人的、几乎不可理解的概念，最终由爱因斯坦借助数学家黎曼和里奇发明的张量的非欧几何，找到了表达方式。到1912年，爱因斯坦已经快要找到方程式的数学方案了，但随后他又转变方向，去寻找一条更基于物理的路线。这条路线只成功了一部分，他只得满足于和同事马塞尔·格罗斯曼①共同发表了一篇理论大纲，也就是1913年著名的《纲要》（*Entwurf*），后来爱因斯坦渐渐意识到，其中包含着重大的错误。

一战的动荡，以及爱因斯坦与科学界同事中德国民族主义的斗争，还有他为探望在苏黎世的两个年幼的儿

---

① 马塞尔·格罗斯曼（1878—1936），犹太人，瑞士数学家，阿尔伯特·爱因斯坦的大学同窗和好友。

子并与他们的母亲离婚所做出的不断努力，构成了又一颗非凡知识分子超新星诞生的背景，这次用时并没有超过13个月，而只出色地花了4周。

1915年6月，爱因斯坦在哥廷根大学做了有关《纲要》的演讲。演讲非常成功。此外，在与同为和平主义者的德国杰出数学家戴维·希尔伯特①的私下谈话中，爱因斯坦解释了相对论，以及他正试图想要实现的目标，还有他当时遇到的数学问题。之后，爱因斯坦公开宣布，自己为希尔伯特而倾倒。他似乎可以完完全全、细致入微地理解爱因斯坦想要达成的目标，以及他前进道路上的数学障碍。

事实上，希尔伯特理解得未免太好了一点，他很快就开始埋头苦干，为广义相对论寻找他自己的公式。而与此同时，爱因斯坦在《纲要》中发现了更多的错误和矛盾。他在10月份抛弃了它，回到1912年以数学为基础的方案上来。爱因斯坦痛苦地意识到，希尔伯特这位杰出的数学家正紧随其后，于是，他开始陷入了确如艾萨克森所言的，"史上最为专注的科学创造力狂热"。在研究理论的同时，他也立刻在普鲁士科学院开展讲座，阐述自己的想法，从1915年11月4日开始，每周一次，共计4周。

---

① 戴维·希尔伯特（1862—1943），德国著名数学家。

在他的第三次讲座中，爱因斯坦当时的理论准确地预测了水星轨道的变化——他写信告诉一位朋友，他"简直欣喜若狂"。就在距离爱因斯坦最后一次讲座还有几天的时候，希尔伯特向一本学术期刊提交了他自己关于广义相对论公式的论文，标题不算谦虚，叫作《物理学基础》。爱因斯坦心酸地给朋友写信道："从我的个人经历来说，这几乎是我所知的最不幸的人间惨剧了。"

和独立于达尔文工作的华莱士不同，希尔伯特试图用数学表达的理论是属于爱因斯坦的。尽管如此，爱因斯坦也和达尔文一样，因为害怕失去优先权，而被激发出了汹涌澎湃的创造力。他在11月28日最后一次讲座中给出的公式，被物理学家马克斯·玻恩[①]描述为"人类对自然思考的最伟大成就，哲学洞察、物理直觉和数学技巧最令人惊叹的结合"。爱因斯坦自己认为，这个理论具有"无与伦比的美"。

爱因斯坦-希尔伯特优先权之争仍在小规模持续。但值得注意的是，华莱士和希尔伯特都很快便慷慨地把优先权让给了达尔文和爱因斯坦。就算爱因斯坦与希尔伯特的友谊在1915年那个意义重大的11月变得紧张，两人不久也就重归于好了。

---

① 马克斯·玻恩（1882—1970），德国犹太裔理论物理学家，量子力学奠基人之一，因对量子力学的基础性研究，尤其是对波函数的统计学诠释而获得1954年的诺贝尔物理学奖。

我们小时候会互相比赛,看谁第一个跑到海边。人们也开展过勇敢、有时甚至致命的比赛,看谁第一个抵达北极或南极,或绕西北航道一圈,或沿着这条河而上,或穿过那片沙漠。有时,其中也包含着强烈的民族主义激情。第一个游过或飞过英吉利海峡,第一个登上太空,第一个登上月球、火星——这些伟大的努力,它们所有的英雄气概和技术成就,都带着孩子气。

在文学中,每个人都是第一。我们不用问谁是第一个写《堂吉诃德》的人。事实上,我们最好考虑一下成为第二人的可能性,就像皮埃尔·梅纳德,他在博尔赫斯的著名故事①中从头到尾独立构思了整部小说,比塞万提斯晚了好几个世纪。世界上最差的小说家至少可以肯定,他会是第一个写出他那部糟糕小说的人。所幸也是最后一个。然而,当第一、去开创、做原创,都是一部文学作品质量的关键。无论多么微小,它必须——在主题方面,在表达方式方面——增进我们对自身的了解、对我们所在这个世界的了解。

但小说家心怀感激地继承了一系列技巧、惯例和主题,这些都是社会变迁的产物。我提到过的自由间接文体,最早是由简·奥斯丁推而广之的。塞缪尔·理查森的小说《克拉丽莎》或许是第一部详尽描述个人精神状

---

① 指的是《吉诃德的作者皮埃尔·梅纳德》。

态特质的长篇作品。19世纪的小说家把深刻而复杂的人物刻画手法流传给了后世。一定过了很长一段时间，小说家才好不容易找到了寓于孩子心灵的方法。在《尤利西斯》中，乔伊斯把日常琐事写成了一首新诗。而且他和弗吉尼亚·伍尔夫这样的现代主义者找到了新的方法来表现意识流，现在这些方法已经很常见了，甚至在儿童读物中也是如此。但理查森、奥斯丁、乔伊斯和伍尔夫自己也是继承者。他们也坐在巨人的肩膀上。

达尔文和爱因斯坦成了"第一人"，声名鹊起、深受尊敬，应接不暇，成了文化偶像，但华莱士和希尔伯特则泯于无名了。这个"第一"，这种独创性，有着精确的定义。不是绝对沿着牛顿学说时间轴排列的第一，而是在被承认和尊敬的公共论坛上的第一。因此林奈学会、普鲁士科学院——的演讲才会做得那么快，还顶着巨大的压力。

19世纪的科学在进化论观点的边缘徘徊了几十年，而且即使达尔文——或是华莱士——没有表达出自然选择进化论的观点，其他人也一定会这么做。每个人都面对着同样的生物学现实，分类学也已经进入了高级阶段。

同样，在20世纪头30年里为经典量子力学奠定基础的杰出一代，如果找不出一种结合物质、能量和时空的方法，那也是令人难以置信的。尽管他们的途径也许和爱因斯坦的不同，而且他们也许没有一开始就通过黎曼张量这种简洁的方法来实现。

成为第一人和具有独创性,在科学中事关重大。实验室竞相争先发表论文。其中包含着强烈的激情,还牵涉到诺贝尔奖。能与某种成功的观点永远联系在一起,是一种不朽。在对这一点的渴望中,科学家表现出对于他们自身作为创造者、作为独一无二的制造者的关注。我们可以从中看出与小说家、诗人、艺术家和作曲家极端个人主义世界的相似之处。他们心里明白,自己完全依赖于前人。在这两者身上,我们都看到了人的一面。

我想谈谈艺术和科学之间的另一个共同点。那就是美学问题。在1858年和1915年,达尔文和爱因斯坦在某种程度上受到了不太光彩或世俗的野心驱使,想要争当第一,这不仅改变了科学进程的方向,也重新定义了我们的自我意识。这一对相距不到60年的革命,代表了人类思想有史以来最深刻,也是最迅速的转变与错位。这种迅疾的速度值得思考。地球围绕太阳公转这个反直觉的概念,花了好几代人的时间,才在欧洲传播开来,站稳脚跟。三圃式[①]与四圃式轮作的伟大发明也是一样。

[①] 又称"三圃制",指农民把土地分成三部分,进行轮作,假如第一块地某年种植小麦(通常是秋播),则第二块土地该年种植大麦(通常是春播),第三块土地则当年休息,隔年三块土地上的作物轮换,三年为一个周期。"四圃式"与之相似。

自从17世纪70年代安东尼·范·列文虎克[①]开始把自己的观察结果送交给伦敦皇家学会起,医学便有了一个丰富的微观世界。但顽固的传统医学却始终对科学置之不理,又过了将近200年,医疗实践才在对有害微生物的了解和抗菌概念下形成。

有一种理论认为,包括人类在内的所有物种之间都有亲缘关系,这是对人性尊严的挑战。物种不是固定不变的,也不是由上帝新造出来的,这种观点一开始很难为教会所接受。然而总体说来,达尔文的理念解释得太详尽、太出色,而且与地质学的新发现高度吻合,因此让人难以抗拒,尤其是生物学家,以及许多乡间的英国牧师,因为后者本身就是很好的博物学家,能够立即领会这一理论的效用。《物种起源》的出版有趣的地方在于,它迅速被接受了。

爱因斯坦的理论是可以被实证检验的,只要观察太阳对星光的折射程度即可,日全食的时候效果最好。1918年起,人们派出了各种各样的探险队,尽管他们带回来的结果似乎是正面的,但事实上,测量的误差幅度太大,无法提供绝对确认。而且与此同时,到了20世纪20年代末期,这一理论已经被写进了教科书中。50

---

① 安东尼·范·列文虎克(1632—1723),荷兰显微镜学家、微生物学的开拓者。

年代早期的射电望远镜提供了明确的证据,到那时相对论也成为了物理学和天文学的主题。

在1859年和1916年,人们加快了对达尔文和爱因斯坦研究成果的接受速度,这无法完全用它们的有效性或真实性来解释。伟大的美国生物学家E.O.威尔逊是这样评价一种科学理论的:"任何特定科学归纳的优雅之处,我们完全可以称之为美,都是由它的简单性来衡量的——看相对于它能解释的现象数量而言,它有多简单。"许多物理学家,尤其是史蒂文·温伯格[1],都笃信爱因斯坦的广义相对论之所以被迅速接受,是因为它的优雅,它纯粹的美,其次才是因为它的经验实证。

那些能够理解保罗·狄拉克[2]著名方程[3](它解释了电子的自旋,并预言了反物质的存在)的幸运儿,会说起它在智力上的胆识和惊人的美。这是一种我们多数人永远听不到的音乐。这个方程和爱因斯坦的一样简洁,人们会发现,它被刻在了西敏寺的石板上。

如果用达尔文的理论来思考爱因斯坦的理论,我们可以推断出,进化赋予我们的对时空的理解,仅够让我们有效地运行机体、繁衍后代。之所以要构成自然选

---

[1] 史蒂文·温伯格(1933—),美国物理学家,1979年获诺贝尔物理学奖。
[2] 保罗·狄拉克(1902—1984),英国理论物理学家,量子力学的奠基者之一,并对量子电动力学早期的发展做出重要贡献。
[3] 此处指狄拉克方程。

择的无情逻辑,并不是为了让生物体——甚至大部分人类——凭直觉领会爱因斯坦狭义与广义相对论提出的各种反直觉见解的。

引力很可能是时空弯曲的一种功能,物质与能量也许存在于一个连续体中,但我们多数人无法将其作为当前世界的一部分感知到。我们是中土世界的进化居民。你可以说我们继续生活在牛顿学说的宇宙中,但其实这个宇宙对耶稣和柏拉图来说也很熟悉。

当著名科学家约翰·惠勒[①]写下"物质告诉时空如何弯曲,而弯曲的时空告诉物质如何运动"时,无论我们是否为之折服,难的是要相应地重新调整一个人的世界观,抛弃这种观念——在宇宙的每个角落都有一个绝对的"现在",那个空白的空间只是一个准备被填满的空洞,不能被弯曲,是一个与时间不同的实体。爱因斯坦理论的革命也许已经重新定义了物质、能量、空间和时间的绝对基础,但我们脑力装备的局限,让我们仍然停留在进化的故乡,常识的非洲大草原上。

另一方面,正如史蒂文·平克[②]指出的,自然选择的分支众多。因此,它们即使令人不安,却也相对容易理解:地球和地球上的生命远比《圣经》所说的要古老得多。

---

① 约翰·惠勒(1911—2008),美国物理学家。
② 史蒂文·平克(1954—),加拿大-美国实验心理学家、认知心理学家、科普作家。

物种不是一次性创造出来的固定实体。它们增加、减少、灭绝，而且这些模式中没有目的，也没有预谋。我们现在无需借助超自然现象，就可以解释这些过程。我们自身与一切生物相关，无论这种关系有多远。我们无需借助超自然现象，就可以解释我们自己的存在。除了继续这样生存下去，我们也许没有任何目的。我们的天性部分源自我们的进化历史。潜在的自然选择是自然法则。我们称之为大脑的进化物质实体，使意识成为可能。大脑受损时，心智功能也会受损。没有证据表明灵魂是不朽的，除了热切的期盼之外，也没有充分的理由相信，大脑在死亡之后仍然有意识存在。

我们有些人觉得这些分支可怕，或是烦人，或者不言而喻是不真实的和（如字面上一样）没有灵魂的，但其他人却觉得它们是美丽而自由的，并且和达尔文一同发觉，"这样看待生命，是何等壮美"，这些恰恰证明了独创性和我们物种的多样性。无论我们属于哪种人，如果无法在对宗教的敬畏和对某种至高无上的超自然存在的沉思中找到兴奋的时刻，那么也会在对我们艺术和科学的沉思中找到它。当爱因斯坦发现他的广义相对论对水星运行轨道的变化做出了正确的预测时，他无比激动，甚至出现了心悸，"就像心里有什么东西断了似的，"他写道，"我欣喜若狂。"这种激动，任何艺术家都似曾相识。这种快乐，并非源自简单的描述，而是源自创造。

这是艺术和科学共有的表现，表现了在完全依赖他人成就的情况下，对独创性或宏伟、或卑贱，又太过人性的追求。

  达尔文研讨会，圣地亚哥，智利，2009

3

平行的传统

那些文学爱好者必定认为,文学理应是有传统的。某种程度上来说,它是一幅时间地图,是一种探讨不同时代和作家之间关系的方式。知道莎士比亚早于济慈,济慈又早于威尔弗雷德·欧文①,有助于我们追溯影响力的脉络。从另一种程度上来说,传统意味着层级、标准。通常来说,莎士比亚占据了它的主导地位,就像婚礼蛋糕顶上那个孤零零的小雕像,所有其他作家依次向下排列。近年来,这个蛋糕在许多人看来似乎太男性化、中产阶级化和异性恋化,叫人难以下咽。尚无争议的是标准本身的价值。定义某种传统,就是提出一个论点,并期望参与讨论。

首先,文学传统意味着一种积极的过往历史感,它活在当下，也塑造着当下。相应地，现在创作的文学作品，也会稍稍改变我们对过去的理解。你不能单独评价一位诗人，T. S. 艾略特在他著名的随笔《传统与个人才能》(*Tradition and the Individual Talent*) 中称："你得把他放到逝去的前人中间来对照和比较。"艾略特觉得，"现在对过去的改变，应该和过去对现在的指引一样多"并不荒谬。我们也许会在安格斯·威尔逊②的小说中看到简·奥斯丁的影子，或是从艾丽斯·奥斯瓦尔德③的诗中听见华兹华斯的回响。理想的状况是，在读了当代作品之后，我们会回过头去，用全新的理解重读逝去的诗人。在活着的艺术传统中，逝者从不会完全躺下。

那么，作为几个世纪来快被遗忘的巨大积累，科学和科学写作可以为我们提供一种平行的、活着的传统吗？如果可以，我们该如何开始描述它？选择和标准同样都是问题。文学不会进步，只会改变。而另一方面，科学作为一种错综复杂、自我修正的思维系统，会促进并完善它对成千上万个研究领域的理解。这就是它获得力量和地位的方式。科学更倾向于遗忘过去。它从本质

---

① 威尔弗雷德·欧文（1893—1918），英国诗人、军人，被视为第一次世界大战期间最重要的诗人。
② 安格斯·威尔逊（1913—1991），英国小说家、文学评论家，大英帝国勋章获得者，其小说《艾略特夫人的中年》曾获1958年詹姆斯·泰特·布莱克纪念奖。
③ 艾丽斯·奥斯瓦尔德（1966—   ），英国诗人，牛津大学诗歌教授，曾获2002年T.S.艾略特奖和2017年格里芬诗歌奖。

上就必然会具有某种选择性遗忘。

准确性、走对路或是其他类似的东西，是最重要的选择标准吗？或者风格才是最终的裁判？托马斯·布朗、弗朗西斯·培根或罗伯特·伯顿的作品中有许多优美的段落，我们现在知道，它们在事实性方面是错误的——但我们当然不希望将它们排除在外。传统必须为亚里士多德和盖伦①保留一席之地，因为他们几个世纪来一直主宰着人们的思想。我们必须留意辉格党派的科学史观——认为历史就是通往现在的单一而正确之路。我们要记住各种被丢弃了的科学玩具——体液学说、四元素、热素、以太以及距我们最近的原生质。现代化学诞生于炼金术徒劳无功的野心。那些一头撞进死胡同的科学家也有贡献——他们为大家省去了很多麻烦。他们也许还会在过程中改进技术，并为同时代的人们指出难点，提供智力支持。

我说这一切，多少是负责的，因为当一位科学家或科学作者带我们去领悟某种强大的思想时，会开辟通往遥远未来的探索与发现之路，将众多研究领域中的诸般现象结合在一起，这实际上是和我们分享了某种特别的快乐。有人也许会称之为真理。它有一种美学价值，在

---

① 盖伦（129—216），古罗马名医。他继承和发展了古希腊名医希波克拉底的体液说，认为人类有四种气质：多血质、黏液质、神经质、胆汁质。

盖伦关于疾病本质自信而又混乱的断言中是找不到的。比如，查尔斯·达尔文29岁时，从"小猎犬号"航行回来刚刚两年，距离他出版《物种起源》还有21年，便向一本口袋笔记本吐露了一个简单、美好的想法的第一缕蛛丝马迹，其中就包含着伟大文学的某些璀璨特质："人类起源现在得到了证实……了解狒狒的人会比洛克对形而上学做出更大的贡献。"

也许最好把真理与错误、标准与定义的争论放在一边。我们喜欢什么，尝过就知道了。直到最近，纯粹的文学传统才不得不列出自己的条件。首先是作品，然后才是对作品的谈论。在某种意义上，我只是在呼吁大家玩一场大型猜谜游戏：科学文学传统会是什么？哪些书该摆到我们的书架上？提出建议就是自找挑战。我已经开始怀疑自己的建议太男性化、太中产阶级化、太以欧洲为中心了。

这是一篇散文——严格说来，是一封信——的开头，关于免疫学。

> 在信奉基督教的欧洲，有传言说英国人是狂热的疯子：说疯子是因为，他们让自己的孩子染上天花，来预防他们得天花；说狂热是因为，他们兴高采烈地让自己的孩子染上一定会发作的恶疾，目的

却是为了预防不一定会发作的恶疾。而英国人却说："其他欧洲人都是懦夫,不近人情:说懦夫是因为,他们不敢让自己的孩子受一点儿苦,说不近人情是因为,他们让孩子们暴露在未来某个时候死于天花的危险之中。"要想判断在这场争论中谁是对的,请看下面这段历史,说的就是这场令英国之外的人提起无不胆寒的著名接种。

这是伏尔泰的作品,写于他18世纪20年代末长游英国时期,展现了一位法国知识分子为英国思想所折服的罕见例子。伏尔泰以优美的文笔在他的《哲学通信》(Lettres philosophiques)——译作《关于英吉利国的书信》(Letters on England)——中写到了宗教、政治和文学。他欣喜地发现这里政治自由度很高,国会权力很大,也不存在宗教专制主义和君权神授。他出席了牛顿的葬礼,惊讶于出身低微的科学家能像国王一样被葬在西敏寺。关键是,他将自己作为科学家和感兴趣大众的中间人,为牛顿光学和万有引力理论提供了一流的论述,至今依然成立。如果你想知道牛顿学说中有哪些大胆和新颖之处,去读伏尔泰。他传递了新思想的激动人心之处,并为文章晓畅设定了最高标准。

2001年,我儿子威廉到伦敦大学学院读生物学的时候,他得到的建议是,不要读1997年之前写的遗传学论文。到了2003年，对人类基因组大小的估计已经缩小了五倍，甚至六倍。这就是当代科学莽撞的天性。但如果我们仅仅把科学理解为一束穿越时间的光，在黑暗中前进，把愚昧无知抛在身后，总是在炽热的当下才是最佳状态，我们就背弃了一段关于奇思妙想和天大好奇心的史诗般的故事。

有一个人，他无比小心地打磨了一些镜头，以新颖的方式把它们排列起来。他从一个湖里取了些水，以开放的心态仔细研究：

> 我发现里面漂浮着不同种类的泥土微粒和一些绿色条带，像蛇一样螺旋盘绕着，有序排列……其他微粒只有上述条带的开端部分；但都是由非常小的绿色球体连接而成的；而且还有许多绿色小球……这些微生物有不同的色彩，有些发白、透明，另一些有着闪闪发光的绿色小鳞片……并且这些水中的微生物动作大都非常迅速，有各种向上、向下和旋转，十分好看：据我判断，这些小生物中，有些比我见过的最小的生物还要小1 000倍以上……

这是安东尼·范·列文虎克1674年在荷兰给英国皇家学会写的一封信，首次对包括绿藻在内的各种生物体进行了记载。他为英国皇家学会寄送自己的观察结果长达50年,而且他把信寄到那里绝非偶然。当时,在一个由伦敦、剑桥和牛津组成的三角小空间里,几代人以来,那里几乎存在着世界上所有的科学。牛顿、洛克、休谟(我想我们需要把某些特定的哲学家包括进来)、威利斯、胡克、波义耳、雷恩、弗拉姆斯蒂德、哈雷:不可思议的天才的聚集,以及我们图书馆的核心部分——它的经典时刻。

有一个普遍的观点认为,宗教和科学处于不同的领域,因此不相矛盾。但我从未被说服。逝者有来生,上帝存在并创造了宇宙,祈祷被同情地听取,善恶有报,这些都是关于世界的各个表述,而科学对这个世界抱有深刻的兴趣。当基督教一统全世界的时候,思想自由的古希腊和古罗马作家大多被中世纪科学所抛弃(但却没有被伊斯兰国家的学术界所抛弃)。卢克莱修尘封已久的《物性论》(*De Rerum Natura*)在文艺复兴早期被重新发现,具有高度的影响力,理应在科学的文学传统中享有特殊的地位。从16世纪开始,人们慢慢明白,对于宇宙学、疾病的治疗、地球的年龄、物种起源或物质世界的其他任何方面,教会的说法都没有什么用处。下面这位伟大的科学家,常被称为"物理学之父"。他因为宣扬地球并非太阳系的中心、并且围绕太阳旋转这一思想,而被认为有着"异端邪说的重大嫌疑"。在宗教裁判所的严刑威胁下,他被迫宣布放弃自己的主张,在软禁中度过了余生。

> 我双手触碰着眼前的圣福音书发誓,我一直以来都相信,现在也相信,而且在上帝的帮助下,未来也将相信神圣的天主教和使徒教会支持、宣讲与教导的一切……我必须完全摒弃错误的意见,不再认为太阳是世界的中心、是固定不动的,也不再认为地球不是世界的中心、是会移动的。我绝不会再以任何口头或书面的形式支持、辩护或教授上述错误的学说……

1632年,伽利略在签字的时候,是否曾经喃喃自语:"E pur si muove"("但它会移动")。我们永远也无从知晓。实际上,他是假装同意二加二等于五。现在我要提到奥威尔,这是为了记住,世俗的权力也对自由的提问怀有敌意。在纳粹政权下,科学出于政治目的而怪异地扭曲。第三帝国为种族优越性理论歪曲达尔文的自然选择学说,为犹太人大屠杀埋下根基。

作为地球上的一种体系,科学本身很难自称是纯粹的客观追求。它的标准富有人情味,其历史纷繁芜杂,充满激烈的竞争、关于优先权的纷争、对窃取知识产权的指控以及权势人物之间的冲突。詹姆斯·沃森于1968年出版的《双螺旋》(*The Double Helix*),是20世纪伟大的科学著作之一。但它对首次准确描述DNA结构的记载是非常个人化的。沃森的合作者弗朗西斯·克里克和莫里斯·威尔金斯(罗莎琳德·富兰克林当时已经过世)也对这本书提出了强烈的异议。

《双螺旋》,以及八年后理查德·道金斯的《自私的基因》(*The Selfish Gene*),标志着我们这一代科学写作黄金时期的开始。道金斯借鉴了几位科学家的作品,创造性地综合了达尔文的自然选择论和当代遗传学,甚至让已经熟悉了这些概念的少数几个人也感到兴奋和喜悦。它加速了进化论的巨变,深刻影响了生物学的教学,吸引了充满热情的年轻一代投身这门学科,并催生了大量的文献作品。

有一本书,对科学写作的发展历史做出了重要贡献,那就是约翰·凯里的《费伯科学之书》(*Faber Book of Science*)。这是一本权威的选集,有着一流的注解。我刚引用的伽利略的"悔过书"就出自那里。凯里在书中大篇幅摘录了托马斯·赫胥黎的著名演讲"论一支粉笔"(*On a Piece of Chalk*),那是赫胥黎1868年在诺里奇为满满一礼堂工人做的演讲。演讲中有一句话非常吸引人:"世界历史很重要的一章是用粉笔写成的……"

当然,赫胥黎又带我们回到了达尔文。除去《起源》一书,我最喜欢的是《人类和动物的表情》,在书中,他阐明了情感是人类跨越文化的共性。他还为共有的人性提出了反种族主义的论点。这是最早利用照片的科学书籍之一——其中有达尔文的一个孩子在婴儿高脚椅上嚎啕大哭的照片。保罗·艾克曼的版本是一本不可超越的学术著作。带着对文学传统的清晰认识,物理学家史蒂文·温伯格在《终极理论之梦》(*Dreams of a Final Theory*)一书中根据当代理论物理对赫胥黎关于粉笔的演讲进行了回顾,为还原论①提供了雄辩有力的实例。

史蒂文·平克在《语言本能》(*The Language Instinct*)里将达尔文思想运用到了乔姆斯基②语言学中,是我所知的对语言最好的赞美之一。在其他众多不可或缺的"经典"中,我想推荐的有:E.O.威尔逊的《生命的多样性》(*The Diversity of Life*),这本书探讨了亚马孙雨林的生态奇观,和一捧土壤中丰富的微生物;戴维·多伊奇的《真实世界的脉络》(*The Fabric of Reality*),其中有关于多重世界理论的精妙描述;贾

---

① 还原论是一种哲学思想,认为可以将复杂的系统、事物、现象化解为各部分之组合来理解和描述。

② 诺姆·乔姆斯基(1928—),美国语言学家,转换-生成语法的创始人,代表作有 1957 年出版的《句法结构》等。

雷德·戴蒙德[①]的《枪炮、病菌与钢铁》(*Guns, Germs and Steel*)，该书将历史与生物学思想合二为一；安东尼奥·达马西奥的《感受发生的一切》(*The Feeling of What Happens*)，其中对情感的神经科学进行了引人入胜的描述；马特·里德利的《先天后天》(*Nature via Nurture*)，书中解开了先天与后天的对立；以及最近哲学家丹尼尔·C. 丹尼特所著的《破除魔咒》(*Breaking the Spell*)，这本书在对休谟和道金斯认识的基础上，为我们展示了信仰的模因论[②]。

从亚里士多德关于公元前344年左右莱斯博斯岛皮拉潟湖海洋生物学的实证研究，到班克斯、法拉第、丁达尔、高斯、卡哈尔、爱因斯坦、海森堡——科学的文学传统广阔、丰富而语种众多。这种文学应该属于我们所有人，而不仅仅是那些科学工作者。这是一部关于智慧的勇气、辛勤的工作、偶发的灵感和各种可以想象的人类失败方式的历史。它也是对奇迹和快乐的邀约。正如我们可以和朋友们围坐在餐桌旁，欣赏电视剧、歌曲、电影，而无需担任演员、作曲家或导演一样，我们应该也可以让科学传统成为"我们的"，

[①] 贾雷德·戴蒙德（1937— ），美国演化生物学家、生理学家、生物地理学家及非小说类作家。
[②] 模因论是一种用达尔文进化论观点解释文化进化规律的新理论，指文化领域内人与人之间相互模仿、散播开来的思想或主意，并代代相传。

享受这一有组织的好奇心的盛宴,这一创造力累积而成的崇高成就。

> 根据《卫报》刊文改编,2006

4

世界末日蓝调

1839年来,世界上照片的库存加速累积,成倍增加,形成了几乎无穷无尽的图像,就像博尔赫斯的图书馆①。如今,这种摄人心魄的技术伴随我们的时间已经足够长了,因此我们可以看到——比如说19世纪末期——拥挤的人群、繁忙的街道,并且确定上面的每个人都已故去。不仅是在公园栏杆旁边歇脚的年轻夫妇,还有滚铁环的孩子、古板的保姆、挺直了身子坐在婴儿车里的严肃脸宝宝——他们都已经走完了自己的一生,驾鹤西去了。然而,凝固在深褐色相片中的他们看起来好奇而忙碌,并未注意到自己定将死去的事实——就像苏珊·桑塔格说的那样,"照片陈述着走向自我毁灭的生命的无辜与脆弱"。"摄影,"她说,

"是有限生命的库存。如今,指头一按,就足以为一瞬间赋予死后的讽刺意味。照片显示出,人们是如此不可否认地在*那里*,且正处于生命中某个特定的年纪,(它们)将人和物聚集在一起,而片刻之后,他们就已经散去、改变,沿着各自独立的命运继续前行。"

那么,有朝一日,可能也会有我们今天所有人齐聚在这个礼堂中的照片。想象一下,200年后,未来某个看客仔细打量着老照片里的我们,把我们随意揣测成奇怪的老古董,觉得我们一心认为自己关注的东西显然很重要,却对自己命中注定的死期与死法一无所知,并且早已作古了。早已作古了,我们所有人。

我们非常习惯于思考个体必死的命运——它是我们生存叙事的形成力量。它在童年以令人困惑的事实浮现,在青春期,可能会以我们周围的人似乎都在否认的悲剧现实再度浮现,随后也许会消退于忙碌的中年生活,再以好比说一阵突发失眠前兆的形式回来。

---

① 指的是阿根廷作家博尔赫斯1944年创作的短篇小说《巴别图书馆》。在这部小说中,博尔赫斯把他对世界本质、秩序的思索投射于图书馆,象征性地表达出他对世界的终极思考,同时也赋予图书馆以崇高而伟大的意味。

拉金[①]的《晨曲》(Aubade),堪称对死亡的最佳世俗冥想之一:

> ……确定的消亡,我们正朝它行进,
> 而且永远会迷失其中。不在这里,
> 不在任何地方,
> 而且很快就会到来;无以复加地恐怖,无出其右地真实。

我们在私下的谈话和熟悉的宗教慰藉里,都要面对我们必死的命运——"那一大匹锦缎,被虫蛀过,发出悦耳的声音,"拉金想,"造它出来,是为了假装我们永远也不会死。"而且我们把必死的命运当作一种创造性张力、一种对我们文艺有利的悖论来体会:被描绘、喜爱或赞美的东西都不长久,作品必须努力比自己的创造者活得更久。拉金现在毕竟死了。除非我们是意志坚定、行事周密的自杀者,否则是无法知道自己的死期的,但我们知道这一天一定会落在某个特定的生物学可能性范畴内,随着我们变老,这个范畴必然会渐渐缩小,直至

[①] 菲利普·拉金(1922—1985),英国诗人、小说家、图书管理员,被公认为继 T.S. 艾略特之后 20 世纪最有影响力的英国诗人。

闭合。

对我们集体消亡的性质和时机的估计，甚至更不确定。不是一屋子听讲座的人的消亡，而是文明的终结，全人类的消亡——它也许会在接下来的百年间发生，或是两千年之内都不会发生，又或是难以觉察地缓慢发生，像一声呜咽，而不是巨响。化石记录向我们证明，大部分物种都不可阻挡地灭绝了。但在面对那种未知性时，人们常会对"末日将近"抱有强烈的确定性。在有记载的历史中，人们始终痴迷于各种故事，这些故事预测了我们全体毁灭的日期和方式，通常带有天谴和最终救赎的思想，被描绘得意味深长；还预测了地球生命的终结、末日或最后的日子、末日降临的时间、天启。

这些故事中，许多都对未来有着极为明确的描述，让人笃信不疑。当代基督教或伊斯兰教的末日启示录运动，或暴力或非暴力，似乎都有着暴力终结的幻想，也对我们的政治造成了深远的影响。天启的思想可能会妖魔化——就是说它蔑视别的团体和信仰，觉得它们崇拜的是假神，那些信徒当然不会从地狱之火中被拯救出来。

天启思想也倾向于极权主义——就是说这些观点是完整无缺、无所不包的，建立在渴望与超自然的信仰之上，不受证据或缺少证据的影响，并且受到了良好的保护，不会被新数据所影响。因此，无意识的感伤，甚至是喜剧的瞬间出现了——或许也揭示了我们本性中的一些东西——因为未来必须不断被改写,要找到新的反基督者、新兽、新巴比伦、新的淫妇,关于毁灭和救赎的旧约定很快就被下一个取代了。

即使只是对基督教启示录浅尝辄止的研究者,也不应忽视诺曼·科恩的作品。他的权威性著作《千禧年的寻求》(*The Pursuit of the Millennium*)出版于60年前,之后一直重印。这是一部关于11至16世纪席卷北欧的各种末世运动的研究。这些教派普遍受到《启示录》中象征主义的启发,通常由一位具有神赐能力、来自工匠阶级或被剥夺了财产的先知领导,被末日将近、随后要建立地球上的天国的想法所控制。为此,人们相信有必要屠杀犹太人、牧师和地主。成千上万身强体壮、受到压迫,又经常忍饥挨饿、无家可归的狂热暴民,从一个城市游荡到另一个城市,满心都是疯狂的盼望和杀人的打算。当局、教会和信徒会以压倒性的暴力镇压这些团伙。几年或是一代人之后,随着新首领和略有不同的侧重点的出现,一个新的团伙又会崛起。值得记住的是,跟在第一次十字军东征骑士身后的贫苦暴民,是以屠杀莱茵河上游地区数千名犹太人开始他们的旅程的。如今,当具有激进倾向的穆斯林宣称反对"犹太人和十字军战士"时,他们最好记住,犹太人和伊斯兰教都是十字军东征的受害者。

让科恩作品的读者震惊的是,从中世纪到当代,末日启示录的思想一脉相承。首先，而且一般说来，对末日降临时间的预测韧劲十足——500年来一次次宣布日期，什么也没有发生，但没有人对重新设定日期感到气馁。其次，《启示录》催生出了一种文学传统，让源自犹太教传统的"神选"幻想在中世纪欧洲长盛不衰。基督教徒现在也可以是天选之人、获救者或是蒙选之人，即使官方再怎么镇压，也无法抑制这种观念对穷人和疯子的吸引力。第三，一个纯粹的男人形象隐约出现了，表面上道貌岸然，声名显赫，但实际上却诱人而邪恶——他是反基督者。在科恩研究的五个世纪里，这个角色往往和现在一样，都由教皇扮演。

最后，天启信仰核心文本《启示录》一书，本身具有无边的适应性、永恒的吸引力和魅力。当克里斯托弗·哥伦布抵达美洲、在巴哈曼群岛登陆的时候，他相信自己已经找到而且注定就该找到《启示录》中所承诺的人间天堂。他相信自己与上帝在地球上的千年之国计划密切相关。学者丹尼尔·沃伊奇克引用了哥伦布对自己首次旅程的记载："上帝让我成为他在《圣约翰启示录》[①]中所说的新天新地的信使……还为我指明了找到它的地点。"

五个世纪之后，美国依然是一片丰饶之地，而且承

---

① 即《启示录》。

担了全世界4/5以上的科研工作，可以向全世界展示大量关于其宗教信仰的民意调查。都是些大家耳熟能详的陈词滥调。绝大多数美国人都说自己从未怀疑过上帝的存在，确信他们会被召唤，为自己的罪孽受到责罚。超过半数人是神创论者，相信宇宙有6 000岁，耶稣一定会在接下来的50年内回来，审判生者与死者。在一项调查中，只有12%的人相信地球上的生命是通过自然选择进化而来的，没有超自然作用的干预。

有一种信仰，相信末世《圣经》预言，相信有这么一个世界：它会被大灾难净化，并在我们有生之年里随着耶稣的回归得到救赎，全民信奉基督，天下得以太平。总体说来，这种信仰在美国的强烈程度超越了星球上任何一个地方，并且从缺乏教育、经济上遭受剥削的边缘群体延伸到数百万受过高校教育的人，再到执政精英，直至权力巅峰。社会学家J. W. 尼尔森指出，天启观"就像热狗一样地美国"。沃伊奇克让我们想起1984年4月全球掀起的那波焦虑，因为当时里根总统表示，他对《圣经》中关于末日善恶大决战将近的预言非常感兴趣。

对于世俗的思想来说，调查数据有一种令人愉悦的震惊和刺激感——你可以把它们看作是无神论者的小黄文。但你应该保持某种程度的怀疑。它们差别巨大——一个调查的90%是另一个的53%。从一个受访者的角度出发，对一个拿着笔记板的陌生人断然否认上帝的存在,有什么好处?那些人告诉民意调查者,他们相信《圣经》是书面化的上帝的话,所有正派的道德戒律都发源于此。这些人想到的更可能是广义的爱、同情和宽恕,而非《旧约》中怀着妒意的上帝所怂恿的蓄奴、种族清洗、杀婴和种族灭绝大屠杀。

此外,大脑有能力进行巧妙的划分。这一刻,一个人或许坚信末日决战的预言会在自己有生之年应验。而下一刻,他也许就会拿起电话,咨询给孙辈上大学用的储蓄基金事宜,或是对减缓全球变暖的长期措施表示赞成。或者他甚至可能会投票给民主党人,就像许多西班牙裔的《圣经》直译主义者一样。在宾夕法尼亚州、堪萨斯州和俄亥俄州,法院已经明令推翻了"智慧设计论"①,投票者也把神创论者赶出了校委会。在著名的多佛案②中,由布什任命的大法官约翰·琼斯三世做出的判决,不仅严厉地驳回了将超自然思想引入科学课堂的可能性,也是对整个科学研究,尤其是自然选择论简洁优美、激动人心的总结,并且是对理性主义者和作为宪法基础的启

---

① "智慧设计论"(Intelligent Design)认为,"宇宙和生物的某些特性用智能原因可以更好地解释,而不是来自无方向的自然选择"。

② 2004年12月,宾夕法尼亚州多佛学区的11名学生家长和"美国民权联盟"将学区委员会告上法庭,原因是该地区学校2004年1月起的一项声明。该地区学校九年级学生在上科学课前会听到这样一段文字:进化论作为解释生命起源的理论"并不完善",而"智慧设计论"是另外一种"科学理论"。最终,宾州地区法院作出判决,认定"智慧设计论"为宗教理念,在公立学校科学课上讲授该理论违反了美国宪法第一修正案。

蒙价值观的坚定背书。

然而,《启示录》作为《圣经》的最后一卷,也许是最匪夷所思的一卷,肯定也是最骇人听闻的卷章之一,在美国依然重要,就像在曾经的中世纪欧洲一样。这本书也被称为《天启》——我们应该清楚这个词的意思,它源自希腊语中的"启示"一词。"天启"已经成为了"浩劫"的同义词,实际上指的是个体用来描述神明对自己有何启示的一种文学形式。犹太人有悠久的预言传统,从公元前二世纪到公元一世纪,像帕特莫斯岛的约翰那样的先知没有几千个,也有几百个。公元二世纪,许多别的基督教天启被剥夺了经典权威性。《启示录》之所以幸免于难,很可能是因为其作者被误认为是圣约翰,主所爱的门徒。要是几近不保的《启示录》也未能留存在我们现今所知的《圣经》中,那么推测一下中世纪欧洲史、乃至欧美宗教史会怎样改头换面,会是趣事一桩。

学术界公认《启示录》写于公元95或96年。人们对其作者知之甚少,只知道他肯定不是使徒约翰这一个事实。写作的起因,似乎是罗马皇帝图密善对基督徒的迫害。仅仅一代人之后,罗马人便洗劫了耶路撒冷第二圣殿,因此被认为和几个世纪之前摧毁了第一圣殿的巴比伦人如出一辙。写作的大概目的,很可能是为了给信徒希望和安慰,让他们确信自己的苦难将会结束,天国将会得胜。从富有影响力的12世纪历史学家菲奥雷的约阿希姆以来,在集合了复杂与分歧的各种传统中,《启示录》一直被看作是人类历史的综述,我们正处于其中最后的阶段;或者完全被看作是对那些最后日子的描述,战后的美国尤其如此。几个世纪来,在新教的传统中,反基督者等同于教皇,或等同于所有天主教堂。近几十年来,这项荣誉被授予了苏联、欧盟或世俗主义与无神论者。对许多千禧年时代论者来说,国际和平缔造者——联合国,以及世界基督教协进会——胆敢通过在各国间播撒和平的种子来延迟最后的搏斗,因此一直被看作是邪恶力量。

《启示录》的演员阵容或内容,在当代的表现形式中,有着儿童电脑奇幻游戏的所有华丽——地震与火灾,雷鸣般嘶吼的马匹和它们的骑手,吹号角的天使,魔瓶,耶洗别①,红龙和其他神兽,还有淫妇。另一个熟悉的方面是数字的效力——封印、兽首、烛台、星星、灯、号角、天使和瓶子都各有七个;此外还有四名骑马者、四头有七个脑袋的野兽、十只角、十顶冠冕、二十四位长老、各有一万二千成员的十二支派……以及最后,最能引起共鸣,并引发了十九个世纪黑暗愚昧的:"在这里有智

---

① 《圣经》十大恶人之一,以色列王亚哈之妻,以邪恶淫荡著名。

慧。凡有聪明的，可以算计兽的数目；因为这是人的数目；它的数目是六百六十六。"对许多人来说，666充满了重要性。互联网上充斥着关于超市条形码、植入芯片、世界领导人名字数字编码的猜测，让人胆战心惊。然而，在俄克喜林库斯遗址①中，有关这句名言最古老的已知记载给出的数字却是616，和苏黎世《圣经》译本一样。在我看来，随便哪个数字应该都可以。人们在对预言的计算中感受到了对系统化思想的渴望，而其中缺失的实验科学基础，则会在许多个世纪之后，为这种人类喜好赋予丰富的表达。占星术也会给人以类似印象：运作在毫无意义的虚空中的对数字的痴迷。

但《启示录》在科技与怀疑论的时代依然存在。没有多少文学作品——哪怕是荷马的《奥德赛》——能在如此漫长的时间里以拥有如此广泛的吸引力为豪。关于这种顽强的持久性，有一个著名的例子，是关于威廉·米勒的。这名19世纪的农夫成为了先知，并根据《但以理书》第14节中的一行"到两千三百日，圣所就必洁净"，进行了一套复杂的运算。米勒列出了各种理由，认为这句话应该从公元前457年开始计算，并且将预言中的一天理解为相当于一年，得出了世界末日应该出现在1843年的结论。米勒的一些追随者将计算进一步细

---

① 古埃及时期的上埃及城市，位于开罗西南偏南约160公里。

化到了10月22日。到了那天,什么也没有发生,之后年份很快被修改为1844,把元年也考虑进去了。成千上万忠诚的米勒派成员聚集在一起等待。人们也许不认同这些信仰,但很可能会理解这种令人心痛的醒悟。一名目击者写道:

> (我们)满怀信心地期待着看到耶稣基督,和他身边所有圣洁的天使……这样一来,我们在尘世间朝圣之路上的试炼与苦难就会结束,我们就能赶上来迎接我们的主……所以我们就这样盼望着来迎接我们的主,直到午夜十二点的钟声响起。这一天已经过去,我们注定要失望了。我们最殷切的希望和期望都破灭了,落泪的感觉涌上我们的心头,我以前从未这么想哭。这是我们所有俗世间朋友的损失,似乎无可比拟。我们哭啊、哭啊,直到天明。

应对幻灭的一个方法,是给它命名——"大失望"(the Great Disappointment)——首字母必须大写。更重要的是,根据肯尼斯·纽波特对韦科惨案①的记载,"大失

---

① 1993年2月28日,美国联邦执法人员出动坦克和飞机,对大卫邪教设在韦科的总部进行围剿,当天的冲突中有6名大卫教徒和4名联邦执法人员丧生。

望"过后的第二天,纽约吉布森港一位名叫海勒姆·埃德森的米勒派领导人走在路上的时候看见了一个异象,突然得到了一个启示:"圣所洁净"所指的事件不是在俗世,而是在天堂。耶稣已经在至圣的天上占据了他的位置。日期一直都是对的:只不过他们搞错了"地方"。这一"神来之笔",纽波特是这么称呼它的,这一"神学救生索",将整个事件带入了一个无可反驳的领域。"大失望"得以解释,还吸引了众多米勒派成员,带着他们心中依然强烈的希望,开始了第七日基督复临(the Seventh Day Adventist)运动——这一运动后来发展成为美国最成功的教会之一。

注意这种趋势和科恩所描述的中世纪教派之间的关系——着重强调《启示录》,末日即将来临,严格区分守安息日的忠诚"余民"和那些加入了"堕落"、反基督者行列的人。等同于反基督者的教皇,其头衔是"上帝儿子的代表"(Vicarius Filii Dei),显然数值就是666[①]。

我提到海勒姆·埃德森事后的神来之笔,是为了说明末日时间思想的可变性和韧劲。几个世纪以来,人们一直认为末日"快来了"——就算不在下周,也在一两年之内。末日还没来,但没人会失望很久。新的预言者,以及不久后新的一代,会开始计算,并且总会设法发

---

① 将该头衔中的拉丁字母换算成罗马数字,其总和为666。

现，末日将在他们自己的有生之年迫近。像哈尔·林德赛这样的百万级畅销书作者对世界末日的预言贯穿了整个70、80和90年代——而今天，生意前所未有地红火。人们渴求这种新闻，或许我们可以从中窥见自己天性中的一些东西，关于我们根深蒂固的时间观念，以及在面对令人生畏的浩瀚永恒或宇宙年龄时——两者从人类尺度来说相差无几——我们自身的渺小。我们需要一种情节、一种叙述，来支撑我们在事物流动中的无关紧要。

在《结尾的意义》(*The Sense of an Ending*) 中，弗兰克·克默德指出，《启示录》经久不衰的特质与活力"与我们对小说更加天真的要求不谋而合"。我们出生，也将死去，都会在事物的中间，在"当中"。为了理解我们的跨度，我们需要他所说的"与起源和终点的虚构一致性。在我们的想象中，广义上的'末日'将会反映出我们不可降低的中间期望"。在面对无尽的时光时，有什么能比把我们个人的死亡与净化万物的毁灭等同起来更有意义的呢？克默德引用了华莱士·史蒂文斯的说法："想象力的一个奇特之处就在于，它总是出现在一个时代的尽头。"就连我们的衰落观里也包含着复兴的希望；信教的人和最不信教的人，都不免把过渡到2000年看得很重要，哪怕无神论者所做的一切，只是把派对开得更热闹一点。这必然是一种过渡，从旧时代通往了新时代——但现在谁又能说奥萨马·本·拉登不令人失望呢？不管我们是在新千禧年的曙光里与下曼哈顿废墟中的丧亲者一同哀悼，还是像有些人那样，在东耶路撒冷开心地舞蹈。

伊斯兰教末世论从一开始就认为，必须以暴力征服世界，在预期的审判时刻之前将灵魂集结到信仰中——这一想法若干个世纪来几经兴衰，但在过去几十年里从伊斯兰复兴运动中获得了新的动力。它一部分是基督教新教传统的镜像（一个完全伊斯兰教化的世界，耶稣是穆罕默德的副手），一部分是对"神圣空间"哈里发国必定回归的幻想，这个国度包括西班牙大部分地区、法国部分地区、整个中东，直到中国边境。与基督教的计划一样，伊斯兰教预言了犹太人的毁灭或皈依。

令人惊讶的是，作为伊斯兰教和基督教末世论的源头，犹太教对预言的信仰反而较弱——也许犹太人和他们上帝之间的关系带有某种讽刺，对末世信仰不友好，但它继续生机勃勃地存在于卢巴维奇运动及各种以色列移民群体中，并且关注的中心一定是有争议土地的神圣权利。

我们还应该在这些东西中加入最近世俗的末日天启信仰——确信世界必然会因为核交换、病毒蔓延、陨石、人口增长或环境退化而毁灭。如果这些灾难仅仅是在开放式未来形成的可能性,或许可以被智慧的人类行为所阻止,我们就不能认为它们会引发世界末日。它们是威胁,它们在召唤行动。但当它们被描述成在所难免的后果,由不可避免的历史力量或先天的人类缺陷所驱使,它们就和自己的宗教对应物有了许多相似之处——尽管它们缺少妖魔化、清洗、救赎的方面,也没有超自然实体的监管,这种监管可能会赋予大规模灭绝善意的意义和目的。显然,宿命论在两个阵营中都很常见,而且双方都有足够的理由对核毁灭高度关注。在先知的信徒看来,核毁灭可以在回顾似曾晦涩的《圣经》段落时得到解释。哈尔·林德赛,美国天启思想普及者中的佼佼者,写道:

> 《撒迦利亚书》第 14 章 12 节预言:"他们两脚站立的时候,肉必从骨上消没,眼在眶中干瘪,舌在口中溃烂。"数百年来,《圣经》预言的研究者一直想知道,什么样的灾祸会在人类两脚依然站立的时候将他们瞬间摧毁。这种事情非人力之所及,直到原子弹爆炸事件发生。但现在,《撒迦利亚书》预言的一切,都可以在一场热核交换中实现!

还有两场运动,幸好现在都被打压或溃败了。它们为宗教和世俗天启之间提供了进一步的联系——诺曼·科恩在《千禧年的寻求》最后几页中这样总结道。天启中世纪运动的种族灭绝倾向在公元1500年后有所减弱。当然，末日信仰依然活跃在清教徒和加尔文主义运动中，在如我们所见的米勒派中，也在美国大觉醒运动、摩门教、耶和华见证会和基督复临会运动中。

然而，杀人的传统并没有彻底消失。它在过去的几个世纪中存活于各个教派与各种暴行间，在20世纪的欧洲出现转变、复兴、世俗化，但依然在科恩描述的天启思想精髓中清晰可辨：

> 人们紧张地期待着一场具有决定性的终极斗争。在这场斗争中，世上的暴政将被"天选之人"推翻，世界将会获得新生，历史将会走向圆满。上帝的意志在20世纪转变成了历史的意志，但本质的需求依然存在，今天也是一样——通过消灭腐败分子来净化世界。

纳粹主义对犹太人的黑暗幻想，与中世纪凶残的反犹太人妖魔论有许多相同之处。还有一个从俄国引进的重要因素，叫作《锡安长老会纪要》(*The Protocols of the Elders of Zion*),是一份 1905 年沙俄警方的伪造文书,被希特勒他们抬高到种族主义意识形态的地步。(耐人寻味的是,《纪要》一书作为伊斯兰教主义者的核心文本再度出现,在网站上被频繁引用,并在中东各地的街头书摊上贩售)第三帝国及其千年统治的梦想是一种世俗化的千禧年篡权,直接的源头就是《启示录》。科恩提醒我们注意《我的奋斗》中天启式的语言:

>如果我们的人民……沦为这些国家嗜血、贪财的犹太暴君的受害者,整个地球将会沉落……如果德国从这种信仰中解脱出来,便可认为是战胜了这种对各民族来说最大的危险,这是为了整个地球。

在苏维埃形态下的马克思主义里,科恩也找到了对古老的千禧年预言传统、对消灭腐败分子的最终暴力斗争的延续——这次是资产阶级要被无产阶级击败,这样国家才能消亡,迎来和平的王国。"富农……准备绞杀成千上万的工人……必须对富农发起无情的战争!让他们去死!"列宁如是说。他的话变成了行动。

30 年前,我们也许可以说服自己相信当代宗教天启思想是一种无害残余,来自更容易上当受骗、迷信、处于科学发展之前的时代,现在已经安全地成为了过去。

但今天的预言信仰，尤其是在基督教和伊斯兰教传统中，是我们当代历史的一股力量，像一具中世纪引擎，推动着我们的现代道德、地缘政治和军事问题。各路神明——而且他们肯定不是同一个神——过去都是直接对亚伯拉罕、保罗或穆罕默德等人说话的，现在则通过每天的电视新闻，间接对我们说话。这些不同的神已经和我们的政治分歧缠绕在一起，难解难分了。

我们世俗和科学的文化尚未取代这些互不相容的超自然思想体系，甚至仅仅连发起挑战也无能为力。科学方法、怀疑论或一般意义上的理性还没有找到一种包罗万象的叙事，足够有力、简单且具有广泛的吸引力，能够和赋予人们生命意义的古老故事相抗衡。对于地球上所有的生物多样性来说，自然选择是一种强大、优雅而又经济的解释，或许还包含了另一种可以匹敌创世神话的种子，在真实性方面也更有分量——但它等待着自己灵光乍现的合成者，它的诗人，它的弥尔顿。伟大的美国生物学家 E. O. 威尔逊提出过一种伦理观，脱离于宗教，却源自他所谓的"亲生命性"（biophilia），即我们与我们的自然环境之间天生而深厚的联系——但仅靠一个人，是无法创建起一种道德体系的。气候科学也许会用根据新数据修正的数字来谈论上升的海平面和全球气温，但说到人类的未来，它无法和耸人听闻的东西竞争，而且尤其无法和《但以理书》或《启示录》中预言的意义竞争。理性和神话依然不安地同床共枕。

科学非但没有提出挑战，反倒用显而易见的方法巩固了天启思想。它给我们提供了方法，可以在几小时之内将我们自己和我们的文明摧毁殆尽，或是在几天之内将致命的病毒传遍全球。并且我们的破坏技术呈螺旋式上升发展，越来越容易获得，已经提高了如下可能性——真正的信徒带着他们超凡脱俗的激情、他们对末日开始的虔诚渴望，能够助推古老的预言走向现实。丹尼尔·沃伊奇克在他关于美国天启思想的杰出研究中引用了一封信，是歌手帕特·布恩写给基督教友的。他的想法似乎是发动一场全面的核战争。

> 我猜，活在世上的基督徒，只要有思想，没有人不相信我们正生活在历史的尽头。我不知道你对此作何感想，但我觉得很兴奋。试想一下，就像使徒保罗所写的那样，亲眼看见"主必亲自从天降临，有呼叫的声音"！哇喔！而且到处都是它即将发生的迹象。

如果这种一心要酿成核灾难的可能性看起来太悲观、过分或是搞笑，不妨想想另外一个人的例子，他离帕特·布恩很远——是伊朗前总统内贾德。他有一个被广泛报道的言论，就是要把以色列从地球表面抹去。他可能只是口出狂言，你在全世界上千座清真寺或教堂的任何一个周五或周日都可以听到这种话。但这种姿态，加上他的核野心，放在他的末日信念背景下，变得更令人担心了。在距离圣城库姆不远的村庄贾姆卡兰，一座小清真寺正在进行耗资两千万美元的扩建，这是内贾德在任期间由他的办公室推动的。在什叶派天启传统中，消失于9世纪的十二伊玛目①马赫迪预计会在清真寺后面的一个井里再度出现。他的再度出现，将意味着末日的开始。他将领导人们与伊斯兰教版本的反基督者旦扎里战斗，并且将和追随自己的耶稣一起，建立由伊斯兰教统治的全球性达尔·色兰和平园。内贾德扩建清真寺，是为了迎接马赫迪。大批朝圣者立刻朝拜了这一神殿，因为据说总统告诉他的内阁，他预计神明的"探访"会在两年之内发生。

或者，再想想著名的红色小母牛或小牛的例子。在耶路撒冷圣殿山上，犹太教、基督教和伊斯兰教的末日故事以环环相扣又互相排斥的方式汇聚一堂，具有潜在的爆炸性——它们也顺道构成了美国小说家罗伯特·斯通的佳作《大马士革之门》(*Damascus Gate*)的素材。

---

① 意为领拜人，引申为学者、领袖、表率、楷模、祈祷主持人，也可理解为伊斯兰法学权威。

人们激烈争论的不仅是过去和现在,还有将来。想要公正地概括挤在这片35英亩土地上的复杂的末世论,几乎是不可能的。这些故事本身大家都耳熟能详。对于犹太人来说,这座山——《圣经》中的摩利亚山——是第一圣殿的所在地,于公元前586年被尼布甲尼撒①所毁,而第二圣殿则于公元70年被罗马人所毁。根据传说,而且让包括圣殿组织在内的各种争议团体特别感兴趣的是,弥赛亚最终到来时,将占据第三圣殿。但如果不用一头绝无一根杂毛的红色小牛作为祭品,圣殿就无法建成,弥赛亚也就不会到来。

对穆斯林来说,这座山是"圆石清真寺"的所在地,建在两座寺庙的位置上,围绕着穆罕默德夜行登宵的地点——登宵时,他在岩石上留下了一个神圣的脚印。在先知的传统中,旦扎里将会是一个犹太人,他会领导对抗伊斯兰教的毁灭性战争。试图为一座新圣殿的基石送上祝福被看作是高度的挑衅,因为这意味着对清真寺的摧毁。阿里埃勒·沙龙于2000年9月到访圣殿山,其象征意义在穆斯林和犹太教徒看来,依然有着截然不同的解释。如果生命不受到威胁,那么基督教基要主义者加入这种反复无常的混战,就会显得愤世嫉俗得可笑。这

---

① 指尼布甲尼撒二世,新巴比伦王国第二任君主,其在位时期是新巴比伦繁荣鼎盛的时代。

些先知信徒们确信，基督将在世界末日大战的巅峰时刻归来，他的千年统治将会确保犹太教徒和穆斯林皈依基督教，或是将他们斩尽杀绝。但这一统治无法开始，除非第三圣殿建成。

因此，在得克萨斯基督教基要主义者农场主的帮助下，以色列兴起了养牛运动，来促使完美无瑕的红色小牛的诞生，从而让我们不得不假定，会把末日提前一点。1997年，当一位有希望的候选人出现时，引起了轰动和媒体的嘲弄。几个月后，这头宝贝小母牛的臀部被铁丝网刮伤，导致伤口上长出了白毛，立刻落选了。另一头红色小牛于2002年出现，引得众人欢呼，后来又让人失望了。在紧紧围绕着圣殿山的历史、宗教和政治中，小牛只是一件小事。但对它的寻找，以及围绕它的希望和渴望，显示出先知信徒中想要引发灾难的危险倾向，因为他们认为这种灾难会带来某种人间天堂。当前美国政府迟迟不愿采取公平政策来和平解决巴以争端，究其原因，可能犹太民族主义团体带来的压力与基督教原教旨主义者的末世论难分伯仲。

人类历史的不确定期、迅速、混乱的变化期和社会动荡期，似乎让这些古老的故事更有分量了。并不需要小说家来告诉你，故事有始就得有终。哪里有创世神话，就一定有最后的篇章。上帝创造了这个世界，就有能力毁灭它。当人类的弱点或邪恶显露出来，人们就会产生超自然报应的负罪幻想。当人们深深失意时,无论是物质上还是精神上,都会梦想着出现完美社会,可以解决所有冲突,满足所有需求。

那些我们都可以理解,或是礼貌地装作理解。但宿命论的问题依然存在。在核时代,以及环境严重恶化的时代,天启信仰造成了严重的二级危险。如果核国家领导人开始欢迎或不再害怕大规模死亡,那么帮助我们度过冷战的岌岌可危的自利逻辑就会崩塌。伊朗11年级的一本教科书赞许地引用了阿亚图拉霍梅尼①的话:"要么我们为伊斯兰教在世界上的胜利握手言欢,要么我们全都殉道,转向永生。两种情况下,胜利和成功都属于我们。"如果我是信徒,我想我会更愿意加入耶稣的阵营。根据《马太福音》记载,他是这么说的:"但那日子、那时辰,没有人知道,连天上的使者也不知道,子也不知道,惟独父知道。"

哪怕是怀疑论者,也能在宗教表达的历史积累中找到快乐、恐惧、爱,以及最重要的,严肃感。让我们再回到菲利普·拉金——他是一位无神论者,也知道超然的时刻与本质。他在《去教堂》(*Church Going*)中写道:

---

① "阿亚图拉"是对伊朗等伊斯兰教什叶派领袖的尊称。霍梅尼(1902—1989),1979年伊朗革命的政治和精神领袖。

> 这是严肃的地球上一座严肃的房子,
> 在它混合的气氛中,我们所有的强迫行为会合,
> 得到认可,并披上了命运的袍子。

还有谁会比死者葬礼祈祷文的作者更严肃呢？这篇祈祷文出自《公祷书》(*The Book of Common Prayer*),像是具有凄美存在感的咒语,在亨利·珀塞尔①的优美谱曲中更是如此:"凡妇人所生的,在世上不能长久,且多受苦难。像花生长,必遭剪割。像影快快过去,决不停留。"

从根本上来说,天启信仰基于信念——那种闪闪发光的内在坚信,无需依赖证据。人们习惯发动理性的力量来对抗不可动摇的信念,但在这种情况下,我更喜欢那种令人愉悦的人类冲动——好奇心,这是精神自由的标志。有组织的宗教历来总是——我说客气一点——和好奇心关系欠佳。至少在过去的两百年里,伊斯兰教对那些失去信仰的人的态度,和对皈依其他宗教或彻底脱离宗教信仰的"叛教者"的态度,最能体现它的不信任。在当今的 1975 年,沙特阿拉伯穆夫提②本·巴兹在一个

---

① 亨利·珀塞尔(1659—1695),英国作曲家、管风琴演奏家,17 世纪最重要的作曲家之一,也是最伟大的英国作曲家之一。
② 穆夫提,伊斯兰教教法说明官或伊斯兰教宗教领袖。

法特瓦①中做出了一项裁决,什穆埃尔·巴尔对其引用如下:"那些声称地球是圆的、绕着太阳转的人是叛教者,他们的鲜血会流淌,他们的财产会以上帝的名义被夺走。"十年后,本·巴兹撤销了这一裁决。主流伊斯兰教对叛教者的例行惩罚从流放到打死,不一而足。穆斯林叛教者有很多匿名交换意见的网站,登入任意一个,你就会进入这样一个世界:满是勇敢而又惊恐的男男女女,已经向他们自己的不满和求知欲表示了屈服。

基督徒也不应该自鸣得意。第一条戒律——关于死亡的痛苦,如果我们要从字面上理解这件事的话——是"除了我以外,你不可有别的神(Thou shalt have no other gods before me)"。公元4世纪,圣奥古斯丁很好地为基督教解释了这一点,因此他的观点盛行了很久:"另有一种诱惑,甚至更加充满危险。这就是好奇之病。就是因为它的驱使,我们才会去尝试发现自然的秘密。而那些秘密我们无法理解,对我们毫无裨益,也不是人们应该希望去学习的。"

然而正是好奇心,科学上的好奇心,给我们带来了关于这个世界真实的、可测试的知识,帮助我们理解了

---

① 法特瓦(Fatwah),伊斯兰教法用语,意为"教法判例"、"教法新解"。指权威的教法学家就经、训或法典未作规定的问题,或法典虽有规定但不全面,或在事实上已难于执行,或对如何执行有争议的问题,根据经、训的精神和教法原理,经过审慎推理,引申出的法律处理意见、补充见解或裁断说明。

自己在这个世界上的位置，和我们的天性与环境。这种认知自有它的美，但也会叫人害怕。我们才刚刚开始理解最近学到的东西的含义。但我们到底学到了什么？我在这里要借鉴并改编一下史蒂文·平克关于他理想中大学的文章：我们已经学到的东西里包括：我们的星球只是大到不可思议的宇宙中的一个小点；我们人类的存在只占了地球历史极小的一部分；人类是灵长类动物；思想是由生理过程运行的一个器官的活动；有一些探明真相的方法会迫使我们做出违反常识的结论，有时是对常识的彻底颠覆，规模有大有小；宝贵而广泛持有的信念，在经受实证检验时，往往会被残忍地证伪；我们无法创造能量，或是无损耗地使用能量。

按照目前的情况来看，经过了一个多世纪在若干领域的研究之后，我们完全没有证据显示未来可以预测。最好还是直视过往，看看它堆满了未能实现的未来的垃圾场，因为在末日信徒认为自己可以依仗着漫长、恒久的千年传统连续体，幻想自己救赎将至、他人万劫不复时，正是对历史的好奇心，才能合理地让他们产生犹豫。网上充斥着无数关于末日/升天的网站，其中一个有一栏专门讨论常见问题。有一个问题是：当主降临时，其他信仰的孩子会怎样？回答是坚定的："对主不敬的父母只会给他们的孩子带来审判。"根据这一点，我们也许可以得出结论：末日信仰很可能不受历史教训的影响。

如果我们真的毁灭了自己，可以设想，普遍反应将会是恐惧，和因为这一切毫无意义而产生的悲伤，而不是升天的狂喜。犹记得我们曾离毁灭自己的文明只有一步之遥，那是1962年的10月，装载着核弹头的苏联船只准备前往古巴进行部署，却遭到了美国海军的封锁，全世界都等着看尼基塔·赫鲁晓夫会不会下令让他的船队返航。值得注意的是，那起恐怖事件在公众记忆和现代民间文学中存留极少。古巴导弹危机催生了一大批文献——军事的、政治的、外交的——却很少涉及它对当时在家庭、学校和工作场所里普通生活的影响，也很少涉及人民普遍的恐惧和广泛的麻木不解。那种恐惧并没有像你可能期待的那样，生动地进入这里或其他任何地方的国家叙事。正如斯宾塞·沃尔特所说："危机结束时，多数人立刻转移了注意力，就像孩子搬起一块石头，看了看下面黏糊糊的东西，又把石头扔了回去。"或许是第二年肯尼迪总统遇刺模糊了人们对导弹危机的记忆。他在达拉斯遇害一事，成为了即时全球化新闻传播史上的一个标志——世界上很大一部分人似乎能够回忆起自己听到这则新闻时人在哪里。克里斯托弗·希钦斯将两起事件合并，在一篇关于古巴导弹危机的文章开头写下了这样的字句——"和我们这代所有人一样，我可以清楚地记得，在约翰·菲茨杰拉德·肯尼迪总统差点要了我的命那天，我站在哪里，在做什么。"在那些危机的紧要关头，天堂并没有发出召唤。相反，正如希钦斯观察到的："它为世界带来了迄今为止最像地狱之门的景象。"

我以摄影是有限生命的库存这一思想作为开头，那就以一张集体死亡的照片作为结尾吧。照片上是1993年一场51天的围攻结束时，从得克萨斯州韦科一座建筑物里冒出的熊熊烈焰和滚滚浓烟。里面那群人是大卫教派，第七日基督复临会的一个分支。它的领导者是大卫·考雷什，此人沉迷于《圣经》末日神学，深信美国就是巴比伦，是撒旦的化身，以烟酒枪械管理局和联邦调查局的形式来摧毁守安息日的余民。这些余民将从清洗、自杀的火焰中现身，见证新王国的开端。这的确具有苏珊·桑塔格所说的"死后的讽刺意味"，就像中世纪欧洲以一位蒙受神恩的男人的形式复生了，他是弥赛亚，是上帝的信使，是完美真理的传播者。他对自己的女性信徒行使性权力，并说服她们怀上他的孩子，以此来开创"大卫派"家族。孩子、他们的母亲和其他信徒都死在了那个恐怖的炼狱里。两年后，当决意对政府袭击韦科实施报复的蒂莫西·麦克维在俄克拉何马城展开大屠杀的时候，甚至有更多的人死去。精神病学家注意到并描述的精神病发展症状之一就是"宗教狂"，这是不无道理的。

所有过去的证据，和我们激发出来的所有宝贵的理性都表明，我们的未来不是固定的——我们在公共事务方面,真的到了觉得这些话是明摆着的、不用再说了的阶段吗?我们没有理由相信,天堂或地狱里铭刻着日期。我们也许还没有毁灭自己,还能勉强过关。对抗那种不确定性,是我们成熟的责任,也是我们采取明智之举的唯一动力。信徒们现在心里应该已经知道,即使他们是对的,真的有一位仁慈、警醒的人格神,那他也是一个不情愿的调停者,因为有一切日常的悲剧、所有濒死的孩子为证。我们其他人,在没有任何相反证据的情况下,知道天上很可能根本没有任何人。不管怎样,这件事谁是错的都无关紧要——没人会救我们,除了我们自己。

佩恩讲座,斯坦福大学,2007

5

自我

有没有一种精神实体像自我一样,如此自相矛盾?绝对地不证自明,却又恼人地难以捉摸。早上醒来,我们一脚踏进它,或是它一脚踏进我们,就像踏进一双舒服的旧鞋子。或者,更准确地说,我们醒来的时候,鞋子已经在脚上了。也有人穿着很不舒服的鞋子醒来。还有少数不幸、病态的人,醒来光着脚,发现自己身处熟悉得可怕的刑讯室。即使在睡梦中,我们也不会完全摆脱自我。因为在我们的梦里,它是目击者或参与者,两者通常同时兼有。我们在定义这个自我方面还有困难。哲学家肯定是这样。描述它和将它传达给其他自我的任务——我们显然永远无法进入的那些自我——是复杂的,从不完整,而且才刚刚出现在我们的文献中,因此我想稍后再以一种有条理的、扩展性的或具有自我意识的方式，在早期现代性的条件下进行论证——这里我大致上指的是16世纪。而且"我们"一词意味着，我的观点普遍以欧洲为中心，源自古希腊罗马世界。

我们可能想把自我和意识本身混为一谈，但我们知道，两者并不完全一致：我们并不总是可以知晓自我的所有部分。意识必然包含对自我的认识，而且自我是意识所提供的一切的接受者，但意识不是自我——或者说，它不是全部的自我，不是自我本身。性格也不是自我。性格具有第三人称特质，可以用来描述他人，或是理解和预测他们的行为，但缺少自我的可被感知的主观特质。有不少不太精确的同义词——心、灵魂、心灵、个体性。"生活"这个词的一种特定含义可能比较近似——比如"内心生活"。这是你醒来后要继续的生活——不仅是在工作或人际关系中的外在表现，也是你不得不活在其中的东西。詹姆斯·芬顿在一首著名的诗中，就召唤了作为生活体验的自我。它郁郁寡欢的叙述者在开头的诗句中宣布："我拿起我的生活，扔进了废料桶。"随后，叙述者在同一个废料桶里找到别人湿透了的生活，把它拿回家，在炉子旁边烤干。"我试了试。很合身。"闷闷不乐的叙述者抛弃了旧的自我，高高兴兴地接受了新的自我。我们中间最不满的那些人可能会抗议——要是自我真能这么容易丢掉就好了。

但芬顿意义上的生活依然不算是真正的自我。我们可以改变生活，我们自身也会随着时间而改变，但关于自我，有些东西是经久不衰或不可避免的。包括酒精在内的休闲型毒品，也许会让你暂时逃避，但你以前的自我，那个你去废料桶之前的自我，还会在你回来的时候等着你。尽管我们每天都生活在自我的界限之内，但显然，它跨出了自己的限制，去思考自身。想想我们现有的语言，是如何以递归形式转向自身的——自爱、自我怀疑、自大、自我牺牲、自制——长长一串，只有我们自己才能编得出来。当鲍勃·迪伦对离去的恋人唱着"你会让我好好跟自己谈谈"时，我们明白他的意思。我们也明白，说话的那个人也不得不被迫充当听众。

神经学家会告诉你——带着曾是牧师特权的自信——你不会在大脑的任何特定位置找到自我，比如在笛卡儿描述灵魂时提到的松果体里，并没有一个蜷缩在里面盯着一切的小矮人。相反，自我在大脑中无处不在，又无从寻觅，散布在极其复杂的神经网络中。但已经确认的一点是，前额皮层的创伤可能会导致主观自我感知发生剧变。损害或几乎抹去自传体记忆的病变，将极大地破坏自我构建，这表明时间、记忆和连续性是自我意义必不可少的组成部分。

现在我们进入另一个争议区。自我作为一种叙述方式，一个我们讲给自己听的渐渐展开的故事，已经构成了当代的正统观念。把这一点写得最好，或是把所谓的"叙述主义者"的资料收集得最详尽的，就是哲学家盖伦·斯特劳森，尽管他仍然对这些主张——或至少对它们适用于所有人的假设——深表怀疑。根据他的记载，对于"我们是我们自己写的书"这一观点，在人文科学和心理疗法中都不乏坚定有力、能言善辩的支持者。这里只列举几个斯特劳森口中的"叙述主义者"："我们每个人都构建和居住在一种'叙述'里……这种叙述就是我们……"奥利弗·萨克斯①说；"自我是一个不断被改写的故事。"杰罗姆·布鲁纳在《被记住的自我》（*The Remembered Self*）中写道；还有的来自其他各种学术资料——一个人"通过组织自传体叙述来创造他的身份"；我们都是"大师级小说家"；"自传中心的主要虚构人物就是自我"。

这种观点吸引人的一个地方在于，它有一定程度的奉承作用。我们是由自己精心构建的，这种感觉赋予了我们力量。美国小说家玛丽·麦卡锡写道："……从某种意义上来说，你终于开始创造和选择你想要的自我。"杰梅茵·格里尔则更进一步："人类有不可剥夺的权利，

---

① 奥利弗·萨克斯（1933—2015），经验丰富的神经病学专家，具有诗人气质的科学家，在医学和文学领域均享有盛誉。

去发明创造他们自己。"

通过写作对自我进行先天、普遍的构建,这自然会吸引小说家。在文学节的专题讨论上,你总会听到我们照例宣称,我们所有人首先是讲故事的生物,我们通过书写自己而存在,没有了这些自我故事,我们就会经历某种精神上的死亡和人性的必然瓦解。但要记住,那些小说家是靠编故事赚钱的。此外,你还会听见来自各行各业的人——遗传学者、建筑师、物理学家、城镇规划者——说,他们特定的职业选择包含了作为人类的基础知识和本质特征。我们都喜欢认为自己不仅重要,而且必要。小说家在这一点上天生就具有自卫性。

我个人很长一段时间里,在这些专题讨论会上,都是一个心怀歉疚却提不起劲儿的叙述主义者。我觉得自己本应该更像个同道中人,热情地参与进来。我的不安源于两方面——一是我对自由意志缺乏信仰,不觉得必须有它,我才能写作或是构建自我。我没有选择我的童年,我没有选择我的基因,我没有选择我最终成为的自我。与此同时,我也乐意把自由意志当作是一种必要的幻觉来接受:我们"拥有"意识,因此我们必须对它负责。二是,无论何时,我记得的东西都不是那么多。童年、青少年、初长成人的时期——都只是零星碎片,并不会按照可靠的顺序排列,只有在努力回想、或是回答集中在这方面的问题时才会想起来,而且肯定不是某种日常经历的"故事"的一部分。我总是在面对索尔·贝娄或约翰·厄普代克的小说时自愧弗如。狄更斯也是一个杰出的例子。他们的小说充满了物料、次要和主要人物、气味、声音、地点,它们都来自他们的早年生活——就像一部关于丰富经历的浩瀚纲目,他们不费吹灰之力就可以把它们召唤出来,写进小说。

和厄普代克不同,我并不记得女生在操场跳绳的所有顺口溜,或是糖果店女老板的名字,也不记得第一位给我检查牙齿的牙医呼吸的气味。鉴于这些缺陷,读斯特劳森的作品,和他引用的比尔·布拉特纳的话,就像是一种安慰,甚至是一种解脱:"我们不是文本。我们的历史也不是叙述。人生不是文学作品。"就像斯特劳森写的:"必须有人把它说出来。"他本人对自我的体验并不是一个自我加工的故事,而是偶发的,有些混乱,由分散的时刻所包围,在一连串的当下中。他声称对自己的过去了如指掌,但并不认为自传体的叙述"在我如何体验这个世界方面扮演着任何重要的角色"。他援引了亨利·詹姆斯的"生活的大混乱"。斯特劳森并未质疑叙述主义者对他们内心生活的描述(尽管他怀疑,它的支持者对自己经历的汇报是否准确)。他只是想说,他和其他有些人不是那样的。

他倾向于把我们按照由来已久的方式分成两类——"一类人对自己的思想怀有原创作者般的情感,而另类人,比如我,则没有这种情感,觉得自己的思想只不过是刚刚发生的事情"。对于非叙述主义者阵营来说,他再次证明了自己是一位善于旁征博引的优秀档案管理员。他引用了爱默生的话:"命运带着我们走过生命的历程,我们看起来严肃而又懂事,就像坐在柳条童车里被推过街道的婴儿一样小。"尽管有着漫长的记忆,约翰·厄普代克却写道,他"生命中一直有一种感觉……那就是我的人生才刚刚开始"。斯特劳森还提到了另一篇文章中的厄普代克,他在文中哀叹了传记作为一种文学形式的不足。它"无法传达在生活持久的现在时中,陪伴在看似真实的自我身边的那种超凡的天真"。斯特劳森无法抗拒(谁又能呢?)弗吉尼亚·伍尔夫《现代小说》中一段常被引用的文字:"生活不是一串对称排列的马车灯;生活是一个明亮的光晕,一个半透明的包膜,笼罩着我们,从初有意识,直到最后……"

众多关于是什么构成了自我的描述中都缺少一个事实,那就是自我的具象化。我们不是培养皿中的脑子。身为自我的体验,同样也是拥有一个处于全部的熟悉、生长、衰退、抱怨和快乐中的身体的体验。吃冰淇淋时你下颌的疼痛,自从孩提时代就伴随着你的膝盖上的痣,只要走路超过几英里就给你找麻烦的脚趾,听到某段特定的音乐时你背上那一麻。或者更基本说来,就是单纯处于一个身体中的感觉——它现在的方位,你四肢的姿态。

厄普代克精于此道，就像他精于所有的细枝末节、"存在感的附属细则"一样。他在《论永恒的自我》(*On Being a Self Forever*) 一文中写道："当我仰望空无一物的蓝天，或凝视着一片晶莹的雪，我意识到有种固定模式的视觉缺陷——我玻璃体液中冻结细菌状的斑点——在浮动，通常不为人注意，在我的视野中。"随后，他会习惯性地、又过于身体化地想起几句老歌，和一点不合拍子的诗句："等待时机的人是我／因为我就是那样一个家伙。"他签名时，手常会在"d"上僵住。他掌心有个点，是很久前留下的，当时他上高中，不小心用铅笔扎了自己一下。抬起左手食指的第一个指节时，他注意到一股淡淡的臭味，不管他怎么洗手都没用。这还挺爽的。清醒时的想法往往荒谬：他的手指甲需要剪吗？为什么他的鞋带总是散开？老调重弹的焦虑，模糊不清的回忆——所有这些数据构成了他私密的自我，他"尚可接受的社会、性和专业方面的表现"下方的基岩。

这些私密的细节，是一个人具体化自我的感觉所特有的。厄普代克在这篇文章中思考了永恒，以及拥有这个自我和它"永远存留，比原子宇宙更长久"的一切独特性意味着什么。他（一个信徒）承认，对于生活环境不断变化的我们而言，这的确有些荒谬。提到变化，我就要面对两种关于自我的对立元素——连续性和短暂性。是约翰·洛克把同一性——自我性——和时间连续性很好地联结在了一起:"要找到人格同一性的构成要素,我们必须考虑人代表着什么——我认为,人代表着一种有思想的智慧生物,有理性,会反思,并且在不同的时间和地点,都会认为自己是同一个思想体……现在的和过去的是同一个自我;现在的自我也还是借助着这同一个自我,在反思这一切。"

有一种关于自我的常见悖论——我们承认自己随着时间改变,我们5岁的、14岁的自我和现在的自我相去甚远,但5岁和14岁的自我对我们提的要求,我们却无法摆脱。厄普代克对它的理解是:"我们老了,把一堆死去的、无法复原的自我抛在身后。"我不同意——尽管无法复原,却从不会彻底死去;即使忘却了,也永远不会抛在身后。一条由原因、结果和随机性组成脆弱的线,将我们与早期的自我系在一起。每一天、每小时和每一秒,每一次心跳,像阶石一样,从学步小儿通往垂垂老妪。一个人仍然会因为30年前犯下的命案而受到审判。我们拥有那个旧的自我,并依然对它的所有行为负责。否则,刑事司法系统将会崩溃。因此,作家在公众场合必须回答关于50年前自己写的故事或小说的问题。这种义务显然是存在的,因为他并没有拒绝那本书偶尔寄过来的版税。但这并不会把他从自己是骗子、冒牌货的感觉中拯救出来。那本书不是他现在的自我的产物。它陌生的句子或惊人的主题很可能是别人创造出来的。所以菲利普·拉金不喜欢在公众场合抛头露面，他把它描述为"装作我自己"走来走去。

最终，在这篇对自我元素的简要总结中，我们要面对最明显的一点——固有的、恒定的、现在时态的思想者或思想的接受者，痛苦的快乐、梦想和欲望都发生在他们身上；用洛克的话说，就是"那个有意识的思想体……具有快乐或痛苦的能力，因此关心它自己，只要是在意识范围内"。它就像感测到数据的屏幕，是同一性的核心，让我们为之脸红，为之骄傲或羞愧，或是像伍尔夫同一篇文章里说的那样，是一个接受者，接受着"五花八门的印象——琐碎的、奇异的、易逝的，或是由钢铁般的锐利雕刻而成。它们来自四面八方，仿佛无数的原子不断倾泻而下；当它们落下时……又将自己塑造成周一或周二的生活……"

我们该如何将这些自我的元素结合在一起呢？试想周一早上，你从家里步行上班。脚下人行道的感觉，你自己步伐的熟悉感，接触到清新的十月空气的快乐。早高峰熟悉的声音和景象。你对交通和行人习惯性印象之外的零星想法。这些散乱的思绪似乎是自发的，但又仿佛依然在你的掌控之下。想到一项未完成的任务，隐约预感到一个朋友会来拜访，一些关于性的记忆或欲望或野心飘过，就像厄普代克玻璃体液中的漂浮物，飞快地回想一下昨晚睡不着的情形，舌头小心探触着牙齿，想到了牙医。弥漫在这一层思维下面的幽灵般的事实，就是你当下的意图——准时抵达工作地点，到了之后必须干完的活。就像之前许多次那样，一个任性的声音、另一个自我告诉你，是时候抛开一切了。趁年轻尽情浪吧！但你不能，带你去上班的那个自我说。你有职责。

也许你会遇见一位老朋友，停下来聊天。你会无意识地试图通过她的面部表情、手势、姿势和她说话的内容及语气来猜出她的想法。最重要的是，当你交谈时，你会看到其中反映出的自己。反过来，她也在做同样的事情。你认为非常私人化的自我，也会从别人那里形成它自己，形成它自我价值的细微差别。

* * *

解剖学意义上的现代人类大脑，满载着它所有的认知荣耀，已经在这个星球上横行了 20 万年，又或许远远不到。我们从头骨骨折和其他骨骼创伤中得知，早期人类生活在暴力中，平均寿命不足 25 岁。但除了个别几个人愿意记下来的东西之外，我们对过往所有死者的个人经历知之甚少。为此，我们不得不等待书写这一文化传播手段的发明，而它才刚刚发明了 5 500 年而已。

对于早期的作家来说，表现个人经历并不是当务之急。破译我们最古老的文本——苏美尔语的、巴比伦语的、古埃及语的，可以揭示出民法，对神、国王或英雄的颂扬，宗教仪式，商业计算，天文观察，洪灾，旱灾，丰收和战争。楔形文字无法让我们窥见任何主观性的表现。我们几乎对古埃及人的内心生活一无所知。

我们往前来到古典时代，看到了一种心理景观，其中，对个体自我的表现可能会被描述成点点稀疏的灯火，就像从山顶上俯瞰到的现代村庄——分散的、不连贯的光点代表了主观描写、亲密人类实质的瞬间。它们身后的背景之中，有战争英雄和他们的事迹、他们邪恶的敌人、道德模范，有与命运抗争的男男女女，有梦想、诅咒、神谕、神的暴怒和可以在诸如《奥瑞斯提亚》三部曲①中找到的宏大主题，有与法律制裁针锋相对的报复。而这样的背景，却将它们烘托得更加耀眼。

有一个有趣的游戏，所有认真的读者都可以玩，因为关于古代文学中这样的人类时刻，我们许多人都会有自己的例子——那是一种观察、一种交流、一种情感实质，它们跨越了岁月，向我们证明了一种与生俱来、经久不衰、超越历史与技术环境的人性。

下面是我个人的最爱——是今晚我要向你们展示的两性分歧三联画中的第一幅。

裴奈罗珮在伊塔卡岛上等了20年，等她心爱的奥

---

① 古希腊悲剧作家埃斯库罗斯最成熟的悲剧之一，包括《阿伽门农》、《奠酒人》和《福灵》三个剧本。

德修斯回来。他回来的当晚,她下楼来到大厅,看见火边坐着一个人。但这真的是他吗?(原文此处为罗伯特·菲格尔斯英译版本)

  一瞬间他似乎……就是丈夫奥德修斯,活生生在眼前——
  下一瞬间,不,他不是她认识的丈夫,
  她眼前只有一堆破衣烂衫。

接下来就上演了有名的婚床之计。她下令将婚床从卧室搬出去。只有在根深蒂固的古老橄榄树上造出这张床的奥德修斯本人,才知道床是搬不起来的。这样一来,他就向裴奈罗珮圆满地证明了他就是他说的那个人。但现在他不开心了,因为自己没有被认出来。悔悟了的她,一把搂住了他的脖子。

  "不要生我的气,奥德修斯,凡人中你是最通情达理的一员!
  神明给我们悲难,心生嫉烦,
  不愿看着我俩总在一起,共享我们的青春,双双迈过暮年的门槛。

所以，不要生气，不要把我责备，

只因我，在首次见你之际，不曾像现在这样，吻迎你的归来……

我的心里总在担惊受怕，害怕有人会出现在我面前，花言巧语，将我欺骗。"

他们和好了，当然。但我们几乎是发自内心地近距离目睹了一场婚姻争吵的动态，一个误解和悲痛的小小铰链，以及它的解决。这并不算是关于自我的深刻描写，但却可以展现一二。这段文字跨越2 700年的鸿沟，传达出了我们可以直观理解的情感生活，一种主观的真实。

这样的点点灯火，主观揭示的时刻，散布在现代化之前的岁月里。别让任何理论家告诉你，18世纪之前没有自我。除了荷马，我们还可以在柏拉图、马可·奥勒留、维吉尔以及卡图卢斯、卢克莱修和但丁的作品中瞥见它们。在7世纪清少纳言的《枕草子》中，一个鲜活的自我初见端倪，因为叙述者感受到了一种文学上特有的羞辱，注意到"有时候，你给别人寄了一首自己很满意的诗作，却收不到回信"。我们在乔叟、彼特拉克和其他无数诗人的作品中感受到了丰富的主观生活。但这些都是瞬间，偶有两三行，将内心生活带到人前。自我显然就在那里，但还没有被当作适合广为探索的主题，还不适合作为文学的主题。简化版的文学史，可以被想象成一个不断拓展可接受题材的故事。

我们得等到早期现代时期,才能发现对那种自我的持续审视。就像在5月,人们也许会看着一片含苞待放的牛眼雏菊渐渐拔高,并且注意到有一朵已经盛开了,比其他所有的花都早。同样,在文化史上,某些个体也远比别人爆发性突破得要早。

这让我想到了米歇尔·德·蒙田。

他活跃于16世纪中后期,无疑是最早将自己作为严肃主题的人之一。为此,他不得不发明了一种合适的文学形式:漫无章法的开放式随笔。他的项目完全是自觉的。他知道他想要什么。当他宣称"我书写的就是我自己"时,他的同代人也许会觉得他任性。现代读者则更容易立刻产生共鸣。"世界总是往前看。至于我,却把目光朝向了内心,凝视着那里,看个不停……我只和自己有关;我不断观察自己、审视自己、品味自己……我在自己身上打滚"。

读《随笔集》,就是见证一个人一手创造了现代性的基本条件之一。在他的随笔《论书籍》中,他声称自己有权谈论超越自己能力的事情。这样一来,他就会更多地揭露自己,而不是手头的事情。"因此,我(对书籍)的意见是为了声明我自己看法如何,而不是事物本身如何"。那么显现出来的自我又是怎样的呢?慷慨、宽容、思想开放,对理论持怀疑态度(在法国人中相当少见),

也怀疑医学界、普遍意义上的权威、神学和宗教狂热、狂喜和异象。他厌恶暴力，在反感种族主义方面也走在了时代前面。他是实证主义者，喜欢交朋友，心态很放松，在生活和人类多样性中享受着轻松的乐趣。他遵从事物的自然规律。"我们都是拼贴画，"他说，"世界上最重要的事情，就是知道如何从自己身上找到归属感。"

《随笔集》是自述史上最耀眼的标志之一。蒙田获得了一种新的方法去观察，观察自己。尽管大家花了很久才明白过来这是怎么回事，但在他之后，却再也没有人走回头路。

我们可能会想，那些散文最开始有没有人看。它们也许给我另一种早开花的植物——莎士比亚——留下了印象。如果你要写一部关于在文学中表达主观生活的完整历史，那么长长的一章注定要献给了不起的哈姆雷特之谜。在历来所有创造出来的虚构自我中，哈姆雷特跳出黑暗，成为了有史以来构思最周密、最聪明、最矛盾、最难以捉摸、最真实、最具体的虚构人物。当哈姆雷特在第二幕第二场以散文的形式说出那段著名的话时，其中有蒙田的影子，甚至是直接的效仿："我近来不知为了什么缘故，一点兴致都提不起来，什么游乐的事都懒得过问……"[①]这里，一名男子描述着自己的抑郁，并说

---

① 译文节选自《哈姆雷特（中英双语珍藏版）》（译林出版社，2018）。

他不知道是为什么。即使考虑到他在罗森格兰兹和吉尔登斯吞面前有所掩饰，人们依然可以从"不知为了什么缘故"那句话中感受到，在一种新的典型现代自我怀疑形式前，亚里士多德和盖伦的旧制，以及他们毫无根据的确定性、他们未经考验的脆弱的知识脉络开始消解。

从某种重要的意义上来说，哈姆雷特必须代表一幅自画像。因为如果不凝神注视着自我这面镜子，就无法构建出如此复杂的意识。1600年之前，没有任何想象中的自我可以和这个发光、卓越的心灵相提并论。即使到了16世纪80年代晚期，莎士比亚之外的剧作家还在创造非恶即善的角色。《哈姆雷特》的主要人物开启了一段复杂、多面角色的悠久传统。这些角色，我们永远无法完整地定义。正如对待真人一样，我们可以对他们意见不一。这种令人费解的程度似乎确保了他们可以存活多年。伊丽莎白·班纳特、包法利夫人、安娜·卡列尼娜、斯蒂芬·迪达勒斯——我们都有自己的名单。

* * *

我在此一直没有区分自画像和对自我的画像。也就是说，没有区分对现存或史上真实个人的自我描绘，和故事叙述者幻想出来的虚构、编造的自我，比如小说或戏剧中的角色。自画像和虚构的画像都为我们呈现出一个连续的、私人经历的实体，就是我谈论过的那种；独一无二的幽灵般的人物；意识和身份的中心，那个经历痛苦、感受情感、拥有记忆、洞察力和化身的"我"。有些权威人士申明，这种自我在很大程度上是一种发明，一种文化的产物，受到时间和历史环境的限制。对该观点最有力的论述之一，可以在雅各布·布克哈特的《意大利文艺复兴时期的文化》和书中下面这个理应出名的段落中找到。他首先提到了中世纪的思想——

> 人类意识的两面——向内的和向外的——都在共同的面纱下躺着做梦，或半梦半醒。面纱由信仰、孩子气的偏见和幻觉编织而成；人类只承认自己是种族、民族、党派、社团、家庭或其他一般类别的一员。正是在意大利，这层面纱第一次化为稀薄的空气，唤醒了人们对这个国家和世上所有事物的客观感知和处理方法，但在它的身边，"主观"也全力以赴地产生出来；人们成为了有自我意识的个体，而且承认自己是这样的……到了13世纪将近的时候，意大利开始充满了个体性；对人类个性的禁令解除了。

与自我是文化的人工产物这一观点相反的想法是，自我在某种程度上一直存在，正如洛克描述的那样——

自我是必然的生物学产物，和意识本身一样，具有一定体积的前额神经容量。哪怕是一条狗，也是它自己疼痛、快乐的接收者。更有可能的是，人类的自我意识一直位于某个范畴中；文化，尤其是它们的艺术，在累积、渐进地推动我们在这个范畴前进中发挥了重要的作用。历史也向我们展示了一些可以让我们倒退的情况。战争和饥荒浮现在脑海中。没有什么比恐惧或饥饿更能让人思想狭隘的。自我向来一直存在——但重点不变：是文化赋予了自我成为我们文学主题的条件。

完工的自画像，或是对想象中自我的描绘，不会向我们展现出理想化的形态，或是我们必须追求的类型或道德模范，也不会模仿出我们可能希望自己进入天堂时的样子，而只会展现出一个个体，除了他或她自己外，不代表任何东西。因此，就像所有人一样，他或她必然有缺陷，也有美德。钻研的作家也必定具备抽离的本领，甚至是怀疑的本领。这种描绘的语言必须完成一项艰巨的任务——合情合理地传达某种内心状态，而且最好展现出随着时间、环境、情感转换而产生的变化。我们毫不费力地栖居于我们所谓的日常生活特质中，但却无法轻松地将它们投射到纸上。要做到这一点，就必须发明合适的文学手段；反过来，自我表达推动了文学形式的发展。英雄萨迦故事做不到。那什么可以做到？私人信件、日记、回忆录、忏悔录，甚至是航海日志，最终是小说。

关于曾被纳博科夫称为"概括的蠢话"的东西，现在已经说得够多了。来看第二场婚姻争吵吧。那是1663年1月9日的早上，塞缪尔·佩皮斯①躺在床上，迟迟未起——这对他来说很不寻常。他经常早在凌晨4点就去附近的办公室。但前一晚他和妻子伊丽莎白去看戏了，之后他们不得不等了将近一小时，才坐上出租马车回家。一觉醒来，他发现妻子愁容满面地站在自己面前。两个月前，她给他写了一封信，表达了自己在这场婚姻中的不快。尤其是她感到孤独和被排除在外。但佩皮斯看也没看，就把信给烧了。伊丽莎白有一份副本，"现在她读了那封信，信写得酣畅淋漓，是用英文写的，写她失去了自己的生活，有多么不快，其中大部分都是实情"。

佩皮斯首先担心的是，她的信会落到别人手里——"要是这封信被别人发现了，那我就太丢脸了，是奇耻大辱"。他接着写道——

> 我恼羞成怒，对她苦苦哀求，随后又命令她撕了这封信。她求我放过它时，我从她手中夺下信，

---

① 塞缪尔·佩皮斯（1633—1703），17世纪英国作家、政治家，是著名的《佩皮斯日记》的主人，曾任英国皇家海军部长，是英国现代海军的缔造者。

撕得粉碎，还从她手上抢走了一捆信纸，跳下床，只穿着衬衣，就把信纸塞进了我的马裤口袋里，免得她再夺回去。穿好长袜、马裤和长袍之后，我把它们一封封掏出来，当着她的面，通通撕了个粉碎。尽管我并不情愿这么做，她也哭着求我别这么做，但看见我写给她的情书时，我就是如此怒不可遏、满心烦扰……

克莱尔·托马林在她给佩皮斯写的精彩传记中强调了这一幕。她选择的题词中，有一段是罗伯特·路易斯·史蒂文森的评语，说的是"那种毫不退缩的——我几乎可以说是毫不明智的——真实，使它成为了人类著作中的一个奇迹。不管他做得好坏与否，他始终是那个无与伦比的自我"。

"无与伦比的自我"作为托马林这本书的副标题，可谓恰如其分。在成为婚姻转折点的这一幕中，佩皮斯细致入微地展现了他自己的愤怒、他的残忍、他对自己声誉空洞的关心、他的暴力，以及他的懊悔（"事实上，我很抱歉，撕毁了这么多我从海上和其他地方写给她的可怜的情书"）；与此同时，也展现出他充分理解伊丽莎白的痛苦，怜悯她，认为她抱怨得对。就连他的朋友，同为日记作者的约翰·伊夫林，也未曾涉及这样的家庭题材。

这又是一个文学主题扩展的案例。佩皮斯确实是无与伦比的自我。他的成熟、他涉猎的范畴、他与政治和社会顶级人物之间的关系、他对当今事件的意识，使他不仅成为他那个时代优秀的记录者，也成为了一个让我们觉得亲近的人，具有冷静的自我抽离天赋。佩皮斯几乎可以被看作是某种关于自我的科学家。他写作期间，恰逢英国皇家学会成立（他从1665年起成为会员，结交了许多科学家朋友）。他所处的社会背景不仅是王政复辟时期，也是英国启蒙运动时期。在那个令人兴奋的时期，世界上大多数的科学都集中在由牛津、剑桥和伦敦组成的三角地带中。人们开始使用"客观性"这个术语。它也可以用于自我。

* * *

我们往前走100年，来看第三场男女分歧，这次的情况很尴尬。那是1763年。年轻人詹姆斯·鲍斯威尔[①]刚满22岁，自认极度渴望在伦敦取得成功。但某天醒来，他却在自己最为脆弱的男性部位体验到了一种灼烧感。他得了淋病。他埋怨自己的情人，演员路易莎，说是她传染了自己。他痛苦地反思了一个上午："难道

---

① 詹姆斯·鲍斯威尔（1740—1795），苏格兰传记作家、日记作者、律师，被誉为现代传记文学的开创者，代表作有为英国文坛领袖塞缪尔·约翰生所著的《约翰生传》等。

我,一个向来只和健康女人安全、优雅地行鱼水之欢的人,会受到荡妇的愚弄?难道我现在要在床上躺好几个星期,忍受剧痛和禁闭的折磨……还必须掏空我可怜的口袋……而且,难道我就不能再和米拉贝尔夫人,或是任何其他上流社会的女人颠鸾倒凤了吗?"而他最近才刚和那位米拉贝尔夫人吹嘘过,说自己"像匹小野马满城跑"。据鲍斯威尔细腻的描述,他的路易莎在他们初次见面的时候,就甜言蜜语地哄他度过了抑郁导致的不举阶段,并且告诉鲍斯威尔,她无法想象离开他该怎么活下去。

他与路易莎对峙的方式,正是他在自己的日记里拟定和规划的——冷静而礼貌。对话以戏剧的方式展开(路易莎:我亲爱的先生!愿你今天身体都好。鲍斯威尔:好得不能再好了,托你的福)。终于,他说到了重点。她吓坏了,告诉他,这6个月来,除了他,自己没和其他男人在一起过。她是得过一阵子这个病,但已经好了15个月了。他结束了会面,从椅子上起身说道:"愿做您最顺从的仆人,夫人。"

回到家中,他向日记吐露了心声:"在整个谈话过程中,我真正表现出了男子汉的沉着冷静和礼貌的尊严,不由得让人肃然起敬……我和美丽的路易莎的私会就这样结束了。我曾经为此自鸣得意,预计至少能安全地相好一个冬天。这的确很痛苦。"

过了一阵子，他写了一封愤怒、恶毒的信给她，向她要钱，支付自己的手术账单："但我想，提到钱，就显得不是那么有教养了。不过，要是我拿到了钱（虽然不太可能），那真是帮了我的大忙了。"她真的把钱寄过来了。最终，鲍斯威尔是这么安慰自己的："路易莎只不过没赶上好时候，当时我还未能跻身上流社会……对我这样的男人来说，上流社会的女人才是唯一合适的目标。"

这是一位野心勃勃的年轻人极富揭露性和谴责性的描写。他用尽了自己微薄的人脉，只为在军队里谋得一个职位。但他并不想成为一名士兵；他想在伦敦崭露头角，成为绅士和名人。因此，他想加入一个不大可能被外派的团（皇家近卫队）。他一想到要睡帐篷或不舒服的床，就心生厌恶。鲍斯威尔的日记最引人注目的地方在于，它们具有高度发达的自我概念——不高尚、不英勇、不可敬，却有缺陷和唯利是图。矛盾之处就在于他在自我描绘中保持着距离，向我们展示了一个人是如何欺骗自己的。

詹姆斯·鲍斯威尔在1762年做了一个决定，要写《我的心灵史》，而我们是这个决定幸运的受益者。他展现了自己的方方面面：在人际交往中风趣、迷人，以他的年龄来说算是博览群书，对乞丐仁慈，时机适宜也会懒散、自怜、无情，一个自命不凡的伪君子，一个夸夸其谈的马屁精,一个急功近利的人,时而残忍,时而滑头,对地位和等级异常敏感,渴望绅士身份。他文笔很好,记忆力惊人,精于观察细节和滔滔不绝的谈话,也同样精于自我抽离。他年纪轻轻,却已准备好要为我们展示他个性的各个方面。他给了我们一个自我。

到了鲍斯威尔写作的时代,有像他这样的先例,但不多。到了18世纪中期,小说作为自我观念发展载体的文学形式,开始确立下来。仅在长长的一代人之后,便出现了简·奥斯丁,而她后面一代,就等来了福楼拜。

* * *

小说在18世纪发展起来,读者也日益增长,似乎一开始就伴随着对主观表现的坚实理解而来。塞缪尔·理查森的《克拉丽莎》出版于1748年,篇幅将近100万字,被有些人描述为文学史上对意识的首次扩展表现。如果没有了蒙田和莎士比亚,这本书写得出来吗?答案几乎是肯定的,因为还有许多其他因素在小说的兴起中发挥着作用。尽管如此,有史以来最伟大的莎士比亚评论家及评注者之一塞缪尔·约翰逊依然称赞《克拉丽莎》是"世上首部展示人类心灵知识的著作"。

英国小说在其早期成熟阶段,是乐于显得"真实"的——真实的记述,被人发现的信件,遭遇海难的旅行者在荒岛上独自生存的回忆录,"在176×年,L某某镇上"的设计。之后很快,在《项狄传》的癫狂喜剧中,它就嘲笑和颠覆了自己对真实的紧抓不放。但还有一种方法,可以为阅读小说的行为赋予一种能力,使它类似于思想本身。这是一种模糊客观描述和主观感受之间区别的方法。只要作者认为合适,角色的感觉就可以影响第三人称叙述。并且这样的角色可以成为意识的焦点,不必局限于第一人称。发明"自由间接文体"这一术语,是为了描述福楼拜的小说技法,但它在简·奥斯丁的作品中就已经完全成形了。从此以后,它便牢牢地嵌入了小说艺术,几乎不会被一般读者注意到。自我通过小说中的自然或社会景观扩散开来。

到目前为止,我没有提过宗教。简单说来,有两个考虑。第一,人们普遍认为,没有什么比与神圣存在的交流更能提升自我意识的。第二,小说的发展及其对主观的关注,很大程度上要归功于新教。

这两点一定都有正确性,哪怕仅仅是因为有那么多严肃的思想者提出了这些观点。但我保留了一点怀疑。在蒙田之前,基督教有超过15个世纪的时间,去培养一种高度个性化的意识。结果乏善可陈,而且肯定是刻意为之。在基督教传统关于神性冥想的书面记载中,真实的意图并不是提升自我,而是在更高的存在面前消解自我。这是谦卑感的需求。当一个人在全能的存在面前感到敬畏时，很难，或者索性说没有必要去思考自我。阅读圣奥古斯丁的《忏悔录》或是诺里奇的朱利安的《神圣之爱的启示》(*The Revelations of Divine Love*)，会给你留下这样的印象：对罪的关注和他人皈依的必要性埋葬了自我。自我克制、自我否定——关键是，一定要远离对人格同一性的考虑。

乔治·赫伯特的宗教诗歌是最好的英文作品之一，但它并不会比弥尔顿的《失乐园》更能引导我们走向自我。我们对赫伯特诗歌叙述者的了解，远远少于我们对蒙田、安娜·卡列尼娜、佩皮斯或鲍斯威尔的了解。但那从不是重点。赫伯特的诗歌更像是祈祷，将虔诚与完美的机灵和一流的诗歌艺术性交织在一起。

有一个机会，如果抓住了，本可以彻底改变西方知识传统的道路。正如福楼拜在给罗歇·德·热奈特夫人的著名书信中写的那样："众神远去，基督尚未来临。从西塞罗到马可·奥勒留，有一个独一无二的时刻，人类孑立于天地间。这种特别的壮观，我在其他任何地方都无从寻觅……"

他这么写，是因为想到了卢克莱修。卢克莱修活跃于基督之前的 1 世纪，早期基督教对他所代表的那种自由探究极不宽容。他的宇宙中没有抚慰人心的上帝，没有标杆，没有不朽，没有超越人类可以赋予的意义。他的传统与德谟克利特和伊壁鸠鲁一脉相承，被埋葬了好几个世纪,消失在大众的视野中。基督教强调苦难和牺牲,而不是自己和他人的福祉,强调没有好奇心的信仰,而不是具有怀疑精神的调查。这些在卢克莱修看来,是为了麻痹人民,转移注意力。它的控制力在17世纪开始松动,即使当时正逢三十年战争期间由神学分歧导致的疯狂杀戮。("只有宗教,"卢克莱修在《物性论》中写到另一场冲突时说,"才会产生这样的罪恶。")

正如亚当·斯密所描述的那样,贸易和专业分工的缓慢演进使人们卸下了持续劳作的重负,赋予他们以独处的奢侈,至少对少数特权人士是如此。他们的数量——我们的数量——几个世纪来不断膨胀,这是一件值得庆祝的事情。只有在独处的奢侈中,人们才能像上文福楼拜信中提及卢克莱修所说的一样,沉浸在"沉思的凝视"中,发现自我。然而,在嫉妒的上帝面前,是不会有这种独处的,实际上,根本连隐私也没有。当然,这并不是说信徒的自我少于其他任何人——而是说,宗教默观的文学传统和这种类型的布道出版物在17、18世纪如此盛行,给兴盛的自我的出现带来了挑战。而这种兴盛的自我的代表人物,就是佩皮斯和鲍斯威尔——应该承认,这两位一点都不谦卑。

对于新教来说——小说基本的多元主义,它令人愉悦的自由和同情,以及如何将"天降神明"融入看似合理的叙述中的美学难题,使它首先成为了一种世俗的形式。比如,格雷厄姆·格林①在《恋情的终结》中让上帝掌控他情节的时候,就是他最软弱的时候(也有人会说,是最荒谬的时候)。

蒙田在天主教的庇护下,乐得过着伊壁鸠鲁式的生活。他厌恶神学研究。人们在莎士比亚的三十几部戏剧作品中苦苦搜索,却很难找到对基督教教义明确、持续的认可——也甚少提及耶稣,甚至是马利亚。佩皮斯和鲍斯威尔生活在传统形式的英国国教中,但它的信条却几乎没有对他们的思想造成任何影响,当然也没有影响他们的行为。我这些早早绽放的牛眼雏菊,本质上都是世俗精神。这四位,照我说,都是美好生活的行家。只有基督诞生之前的时代或是现代才能容得下他们。

如今,在西方的知识堡垒中,我们多数是不信神的,而且不管愿不愿意,大多通过各种哲学唯物主义,变成了德谟克利特、伊壁鸠鲁和卢克莱修传统的继承者。就连那些对科学毫不关心的人,吸收的科学世界观也比他们可能愿意承认的更多。在我看来,17世纪及18世纪早期,科学和哲学合二为一的时候,正是我们伟大而缓慢的转折点。

---

① 格雷厄姆·格林(1904—1991),英国作家、编剧、文学评论家。一生获得21次诺奖提名,被誉为"诺贝尔文学奖无冕之王"。

从那时起，自我意识得到了传播，但未必有所增长。我们在"认识你自己"方面尚未取得很大的进步。我们也许有了集体的自我意识，但遇到我们集体引发的事件时，还是无能为力。尽管我们有那么多的科技，迷信也在消退，可依然如此。然而，我们的文学，正如前文鲍勃·迪伦所唱，依然是我们与自我好好对话的过程。

即使我们将大脑等同于思想，我们依然会惊讶于自我可以从单纯的物质中产生，并描绘它自己，惊讶于自我并不是思想的原因，而是产物。至少在西欧，我们许多人已经回到了福楼拜发现的那个空间——在罗马众神死后、基督降临之前。我们失去了抚慰人心的神，可也摆脱了他的支配。我们的时代更艰难，但更有趣。我们也许都会聚集在帕特农神庙这样的旅游景点前，拿着智能手机自拍；在当代身份政治和性取向运动中，我们都应该礼貌地让人们做自己想做的人，过自己想过的生活——但我们所有人和哈姆雷特一样，在面对这个"泥土塑成的生命"时，最终还是要独自应对自我，我们的自我。

Science

IAN McEWAN

Contents

1. Literature, Science and Human Nature   127
2. The Originality of the Species   159
3. A Parallel Tradition   180
4. End of the World Blues   192
5. The Self   225

1

Literature, Science and Human Nature

GREATNESS IN LITERATURE is more intelligible and amenable to most of us than greatness in science. All of us have an idea, our own, or one that has been imposed upon us, of what is meant by a great novelist. Whether it is in a spirit of awe and delight, duty or scepticism, we grasp at first hand, when we read *Anna Karenina*, or *Madame Bovary*, what people mean when they speak of greatness. We have the privilege of unmediated contact. From the first sentence, we come into a presence, and we can see for ourselves the quality of a particular mind; in a matter of minutes we may read the fruits of a long forgotten afternoon, an afternoon's work done in isolation, a hundred and fifty years ago. And what was once an unfolding personal secret, is now ours. Imaginary people appear before us, their historical and domestic circumstances are very particular, their characters equally so. We witness and judge the skill with which they are conjured.

By an unspoken agreement, a kind of contract between writer and reader, it is assumed that however strange these people are, we will understand them readily enough to be able to appreciate their strangeness. To do this, we must bring our own general understanding of what it means to be a person. We have, in the terms of cognitive psychology, a theory of mind, a more or less automatic understanding of what it means to be someone else. Without this understanding, as the psychopathology shows, we would find it virtually impossible to form and sustain relationships, read expressions or intentions, or perceive how we ourselves are understood. To the particular instances that are presented to us in a novel, we bring this deep and broad understanding. When Saul Bellow's Herzog stands in front of a mirror, as characters in fiction so often and conveniently do, he is wearing only a newly purchased straw hat and underpants. His mother

> wanted him to become a rabbi, and he seemed to himself gruesomely unlike a rabbi now in the trunks and straw hat, his face charged with heavy sadness, foolish utter longing of which a religious life might have purged him. That mouth! – heavy

with desire and irreconcilable anger, the straight nose sometimes grim, the dark eyes! And his figure! – the long veins winding in the arms and filling in the hanging hands, an ancient system, of greater antiquity than the Jews themselves... Bare-legged, he looked like a Hindu.

A reader may not understand from the inside every specific of Herzog's condition – a mid-twentieth-century American, a Jew, a city dweller, a divorcé, an alienated intellectual, and nor might a young reader sympathise with the remorse of early middle age, but self-scrutiny that is edging towards a reckoning has a general currency, as does the droll, *faux naïf* perception that one's biology – the circulatory system – predates and, by implication, is even more of the essence of being human, than one's religion. Literature flourishes along the channels of this unspoken agreement between writers and readers, offering a mental map whose north and south are the specific and the general. At its best, literature is universal, illuminating human nature at precisely the point at which it is most parochial and specific.

Greatness in science is harder for most of us to grasp. We can make a list of scientists we've been told are great, but few of us have had the kind of intimate contact that would illuminate the particular qualities of any particular achievement. Partly, it's the work itself: it doesn't invite us in – it's objectifying, therefore distancing, corrupted by difficult or seemingly irrelevant detail. Mathematics is also a barrier. Furthermore, scientific ideas happily float free of their creators. Scientists might know the classical Laws of Motion but have never read Newton on the matter, or have grasped relativity from text books without reading Einstein's Special or General Theories, or know the structure of DNA without having – or needing – a first-hand knowledge of Crick and Watson's 1953 paper.

Here is a rare case in point. Their 1953 paper, a mere twelve hundred words, published in the journal *Nature*, ended with the famously modest conclusion: 'It has not escaped our notice that the specific pairing we have postulated immediately suggests a possible copying mechanism for the genetic material.' 'It has not escaped our notice . . .': the drawing-room politesse of the double negative is touchingly transparent. It roughly translates as, 'Look at us, everybody! We've found the mechanism by which life on earth replicates, we're excited as hell and can't sleep a wink.' 'It has not escaped our notice' is the kind of close contact I mean. In a scientific paper it is not often encountered at first hand.

However, there is one pre-eminent scientist who is almost as approachable in this respect as a novelist. It's perfectly possible for the non-scientist to understand what it is in Darwin's work which makes him unique and great. In part, it is the sequence of benign accidents that set him on his course, each step to be measured against the final achievement. And partly it's the subject itself. Natural history, or nineteenth-century biology generally, was a descriptive science. The theory of natural selection is not, in its essentials, difficult to understand, though its implications have been vast, its applications formidable and its elaborations in scientific terms quite complex – as the computational biology of William Hamilton shows. Partly, too, because Darwin, though not the greatest prose writer of the nineteenth century, was intensely communicative, affectionate, intimate and honest. He wrote many letters, and filled many notebooks.

Let us read his life as a novel, like Herzog, driving forwards towards a great reckoning. The sixteen-year-old Charles is at university in Edinburgh and beginning to show disillusionment with the study of medicine. He writes to his sisters that 'I am going to learn to stuff birds, from a blackamoor.' Charles takes his lessons in taxidermy from one John Edmonstone, a freed slave, and found his teacher 'very pleasant and intelligent'. Edmonstone recounts to the young Darwin his experiences as a slave, and describes the wonders of a tropical rainforest. All his life, Darwin was to abhor slavery, and this early acquaintanceship may have had some bearing on the relatively neglected book of Darwin's I want to discuss. The following year Darwin comes in contact with the evolutionary ideas of Lamarck, and in the Edinburgh debating societies hears passionate, godless arguments for scientific materialism. He spends days foraging along the shores of the Firth of Forth looking for sea creatures, and an 1827 notebook records detailed observations of two marine invertebrates.

Since Charles does not warm to the prospect of becoming a physician, his father 'proposed that I should become a clergyman. He was very properly vehement against my turning an idle sporting man, which then seemed my probable destination.' So he studies at Cambridge where, at the age of eighteen, his love of natural history is becoming a passion. 'What fun we will have together,' he writes to his cousin, 'what beetles we will catch, it will do my heart good to go once more together to some of our old haunts . . . we will make regular campaigns into the Fens; Heaven protect the beetles.' And in another letter, 'I am dying by inches from not having anybody to talk to about insects.' In his last two terms, his mentor Henslowe, Professor of Botany, persuades him to take up geology.

After Cambridge, the offer comes through Henslow

to be the naturalist and companion to the captain on board the *Beagle*, making a government survey of South America. We may follow the wrangling as he persuades his father, with the help of Uncle Josiah Wedgewood. 'I must state again,' implores the earnest Charles, 'I cannot think it would unfit me hereafter for a steady life.' Many weeks of delay, then, after two false starts, he sets sail on 27 December 1831. Days of seasickness, then the *Beagle* is prevented by quarantine measures from landing in La Palma in the Canaries. But Charles has a net in the stern of the ship, the weather is fine and he catches 'a great number of curious animals, and fully occupied my time in my cabin'. Finally, landfall at St Jago in the Cape Verde islands, and the young man is in ecstasy. 'The island has given me so much instruction and delight,' he writes to his father; 'it is utterly useless to say anything about the scenery – it would be as profitable to explain to a blind man colours, as to person who has not been out of Europe, the total dissimilarity of a tropical view . . . Whenever I enjoy anything I always look forward to writing it down . . . So you must excuse raptures and those raptures badly expressed.'

He enjoys working in his cramped cabin, drawing and describing his specimens of rocks, plants and animals and preserving them to send them back to England, to Henslow. The enthusiasm does not die as the expedition proceeds, but to it is added a growing scientific confidence. He writes to Henslowe,

> nothing has so much interested me as finding two species of elegantly coloured Planariae, inhabiting the dry forest! The false relation they bear to snails is the most extraordinary thing of the kind I have ever seen ... some of the marine species possess an organisation so marvellous that I can scarcely credit my eyesight ... Today I have been out and returned like Noah's Ark, with animals of all sorts ... I have found a most curious snail, and spiders, beetles, snakes, scorpions *ad libitum*. And to conclude, shot a Cavia weighing one hundredweight ...

With vast quantities of his preserved specimens preceding him, and already being described, and with his own theories about the formation of the earth, and of coral reefs, taking shape in his mind, Darwin arrives back in England five years later, at the age of twenty-seven, already a scientist of some standing. There is something of the thrill and illumination of great literature when Darwin, at the age of twenty nine, only two years after he had returned from his voyage on the *Beagle*, and still twenty-one years before he would publish *On the Origin of Species*, confides to a pocket notebook the first hints of a simple, beautiful idea: 'Origin of man now proved . . . He who understands baboon would do more towards metaphysics than Locke.'

And yet *On the Origin of Species* itself does not allow an easy route into an understanding of Darwin's greatness. Read as a book rather than as a theory, it can overwhelm the non-specialist reader with a proliferation of instances – the fruits of Darwin's delay – and it's significant that the most frequently quoted passages occur in the final paragraphs.

Darwin was the sort of scientist whose work permeated his life. His later study of the earthworms in the garden at Downe is well known. He attended country markets to quiz horse, dog and pig breeders, and at country shows he sought out growers of prize vegetables. Always a warmly devoted father, he recorded in a notebook, 'My first child was born on December 27th 1839, and I at once commenced to make notes on the first dawn of the various expressions which he exhibited . . .' Long before an innate theory of mind had been postulated, Darwin was experimenting with his eldest child, William, and reaching his own conclusions:

> When [William was] a few days over six months old, his nurse pretended to cry, and I saw that his face instantly assumed a melancholy expression, with the corners of the mouth strongly depressed.

> Therefore it seems to me that an innate feeling must have told him that the pretended crying of his nurse expressed grief; and this, through the instinct of sympathy, excited grief in him.

While out riding, he stops to talk to a woman, and notes the contraction in her brows as she looks up at him with the sun at his back. At home he takes three of his children out into the garden and gets them to look up at a bright portion of the sky. The reason? 'With all three, the orbicular, corrugator and pyramidal muscles were energetically contracted, through reflex action . . .'

Over many years, while engaged in other work, Darwin was researching *The Expression of the Emotions in Man and Animals*, his most extraordinary and approachable book, rich in observed detail and brilliant speculation, beautifully illustrated – one of the first scientific books to use photographs, including some of his own baby pouting and laughing – and available in a third edition, prepared and annotated by the American psychologist of the emotions, Paul Ekman. Darwin not only sets out to describe expressions in dogs and cats as well as man – how we contract the muscles around our eyes when we are angry and reveal our canine teeth, and how, in Ekman's words, we want to touch with our faces those we love; he also poses the difficult question,

Why? Why do we redden with embarrassment rather than go pale? Why do the inner corners of the brow lift in sorrow, and not the whole brow? Why do cats arch their backs in affection? An emotion, he argued, was a physiological state, a direct expression of physiological change. In pursuit of these questions, there are numerous pleasing digressions and observations: the way a billiard player, especially a novice, tries to guide the ball towards its target with a movement of the head, or even the whole body. How a cross child sitting on its parent's knee raises one shoulder and gives a backward push with it in an expression of rejection; the firm closure of the mouth during a delicate or difficult operation.

Behind this wealth of detail lay more basic questions. Do we *learn* to smile when we are happy, or is the smile innate? In other words, are expressions universal to all cultures and races, or are they culture-specific? He wrote to people in remote corners of the British Empire asking them to observe the expressions of the indigenous populations. In England he showed photographs of various expressions and asked people to comment on them. He drew on his own experience. The book is anecdotal, unscientific and very clear-sighted. The expressions of emotion are the products of evolution, Darwin concluded, and therefore universal. He opposed the influential views of the anatomist Sir Charles Bell that certain unique muscles, with no equivalent in the animal kingdom, had been created by God in the faces of men to allow them to communicate their feelings to one another. In a footnote, Ekman quotes from Bell's book: 'the most remarkable muscle in the human face is the corrugator supercilii which knits the eyebrows with an enigmatic effect which unaccountably but irresistibly conveys the idea of mind.' In Darwin's copy of Bell's book, he has underlined the passage and written, 'I suspect he never dissected monkey.' Of course, these muscles, as Darwin showed, existed in other primates.

By showing that the same principles governing expression applied in primates and man, Darwin argued for continuity and gradation of species – important generally to his theory of evolution, and to disproving the Christian view that man was a special creation, set apart from all other animals. He was intent too on demonstrating, through universality, a common descent for all races of mankind. In this he opposed himself forcefully to the racist views of scientists like Agassiz, who argued that Africans were inferior to Europeans because they were descended from a different and inferior stock. In a letter to Hooker, Darwin mentions how Agassiz had been maintaining the doctrine of 'several species' (i.e. of man), 'much, I daresay, to the comfort of slave-holding Southerns'.

Modern palaeontology and molecular biology show Darwin to have been right, and Agassiz wrong: we are descended from a common stock of anatomically modern humans who migrated out of East Africa perhaps as recently as 200,000 years ago and spread around the world. Local differences in climate have produced variations in the species that are in many cases literally skin-deep. We have fetishised these differences to rationalise conquest and subjugation. As Darwin puts it:

> all the chief expressions exhibited by man are the same throughout the world. This fact is interesting as it affords a new argument in favour of the several races being descended from a single parent stock, which must have been almost completely human in structure, and to a large extent, in mind, before the period at which the races diverged from each other.

We should be clear about what is implied by the universal expressions of emotion. The eating of a snail or a piece of cheddar cheese may give rise to delight in one culture and disgust in another. But disgust, regardless of the cause, has a universal expression. In Darwin's words: 'The mouth is opened widely, with the upper lip strongly retracted, which wrinkles the side of the nose.' The expression and the physiology are products of evolution. But emotions are also, of course, shaped by culture. Our ways of managing our emotions, our attitudes to them, the way we describe them, are learned and differ from culture to culture. Still, behind the notion of a commonly held stock of emotion lies that of a universal human nature. And until fairly recently, and for a good part of the twentieth century, this has been a reviled notion. Darwin's book was out of favour for a long time after his death. The climate of opinion has changed now, and Ekman's superb edition was a major publishing event and has been enthusiastically welcomed.

As must be clear by now, I think that the exercise of imagination and ingenuity as expressed in literature supports Darwin's view. It would not be possible to read and enjoy literature from a time remote from our own, or from a culture that was profoundly different from our own, unless we shared some common emotional ground, some deep reservoir of assumptions, with the writer. An annotated edition that clarifies matters of historical circumstance or local custom or language is always useful, but it's never fundamentally necessary to a reading. What we have in common with each other is just as extraordinary in its way as all our exotic differences.

I mentioned earlier the parochial and the universal as polarities in literature. One might think of literature as encoding both our cultural and genetic inheritance. Each of these two elements, genes and culture, has had a reciprocal shaping effect, for as primates we are intensely social creatures, and our social environment has exerted over time a powerful adaptive pressure. This gene-culture co-evolution, elaborated by E. O. Wilson among others, dissolves the oppositions of nature versus nurture. If one reads accounts of the systematic non-intrusive observations of troupes of bonobo – bonobos and common chimps rather than Darwin's baboons are our closest relatives – one might see rehearsed all the major themes of the English nineteenth-century novel: alliances made and broken, individuals rising while others fall, plots hatched, revenge, gratitude, injured pride, successful and unsuccessful courtship, bereavement and mourning. Approximately five million years separate us and the bonobos from our common ancestor – and given that a lot of this coming and going is ultimately about sex (I'm talking here about bonobos *and* the nineteenth-century novel) that is a long time during which, cumulatively, successful social strategies effect the distribution of certain genes and not others.

That we have a nature, that its values are self-evident to us to the point of invisibility, and that it would be a different nature if we were, say, termites, was the case E. O. Wilson was making when he conjured a highly educated 'Dean of Termitities', who delivers a stirring commencement day address to his fellow termites:

> Since our ancestors, the macrotermitine termites, achieved 10 kilogram weight and larger brains during their rapid evolution through the later Tertiary period and learned to write with pheromone script, termitistic scholarship has refined ethical philosophy. It is now possible to express the de-ontological imperatives of moral behaviour with precision. These imperatives are mostly self-evident and universal. They are the very essence of termitity. They include the love of darkness and of the deep saprophytic, basidiomycetic penetralia of the soil; the centrality of colony life amidst a richness of war and trade among the colonies; the sanctity of the physiological caste system; the evil of personal reproduction by worker castes; the mystery of deep love for reproductive siblings, which turns to hatred the instant they mate; rejection of the evil of personal rights; the infinite aesthetic pleasure of pheromenal song; the aesthetic pleasure of eating from nestmates' anuses after the shedding of the skin; the joy of cannibalism and surrender of the body for consumption when sick or injured ... Some termitistically inclined scientists, particularly the ethologists and sociobiologists, argue that

our social organisation is shaped by our genes and that our ethical precepts simply reflect the peculiarities of termite evolution. They assert that ethical philosophy must take into account the structure of the termite brain and the evolutionary history of the species. Socialisation is genetically channelled and some forms of it all but inevitable. This proposal has created major academic controversy...

That is to say, whether it's a saga, a concrete poem, a Bildungsroman or a haiku, and regardless of when it was written and in what colony, you would just *know* a piece of termite literature as soon as you had read a line or two. Extrapolating from the termite literary tradition, we can say that our own human literature does not define human nature so much as exemplify it.

If there are human universals that transcend culture, then it follows that they do not change, or they do not change easily. And if something does change in us historically, then by definition it is not human nature that has changed, but some characteristic special to a certain time and circumstance. And yet there are writers who like to make their point by assuming that human nature is a frail entity, subject to sudden lurches – exciting revolutionary improvements or deeply regrettable deterioration, and defining the moment of the change has always been an irresistible intellectual pursuit. No one, I think, has yet exceeded Virginia Woolf for precision in this matter, though she does allow a certain ironic haziness about the actual date: 'On or about December 1910', she wrote in her essay 'Character in Fiction', 'human character changed.' Woolf of course was preoccupied with the great gulf, as she saw it, that separated her generation from her parents'. The famous anecdote may or may not be true, but one hopes it was. It has Lytton Strachey entering a drawing room in 1908, encountering Virginia and her sister, pointing to a stain on Vanessa's dress and enquiring, 'Semen?' 'With that one word', Virginia wrote, 'all barriers of reticence and reserve went down.' The nineteenth century had officially ended. The world would never be the same again.

I remember similar apocalyptic generational claims made in the sixties and early seventies. Human nature changed forever, it was claimed at the time, in a field near Woodstock in 1967, or in the same year with the release of *Sergeant Pepper*, or the year before on a certain undistinguished street in San Francisco. The Age of Aquarius had dawned, and things would never be the same again.

Less light-headed than Virginia Woolf, but equally definitive, was T. S. Eliot in his essay 'The Metaphysical Poets'. He discovered that in the seventeenth century 'a dissociation of sensibility set in, from which we have never recovered'. He was, of course, speaking of English poets, who 'possessed a mechanism of sensibility which could devour any kind of experience', but I think we can assume that he thought they generally shared a biology with other people. His theory, which, as he conceded, was perhaps too brief to carry conviction, expresses both Eliot's regret (this dissociation was not a good thing) and his hopes (this dissociation could be reversed by those modern poets who would redefine modern sensibilities to his prescription).

Jacob Burkhardt, defining his own choice moment in *The Civilisation of the Renaissance in Italy*, discerned a blossoming, not simply in human nature, but in consciousness itself: 'In the Middle Ages', he wrote,

> both sides of human consciousness – that which was turned within as that which was turned without – lay dreaming or half-awake beneath a common veil. Man was conscious of himself only as a member of a race, people, party, family, or corporation... But at the close of the thirteenth century, Italy began to swarm with individuality; the ban laid upon human personality was dissolved.

The French historian Philippe Aries defined a radical shift in human emotions in the eighteenth century when parents began to feel a self-conscious love for their children. Before then, a child was little more than a tiny, incapable adult, likely to be carried off by disease and therefore not worth investing with too much feeling. A thousand medieval tombstones and their heartfelt inscriptions to a departed child may have provided the graveyard for this particular theory, but Aries' work demonstrates a secondary or parallel ambition in the pursuit of the defining moment of change in human nature – that is, the aim of locating the roots of our modernity. This is more or less central to the project of intellectual history – to ask at which moment, in which set of circumstances, we became recognisable to ourselves. At least some of these candidates will be familiar to you: the invention of agriculture 10,000 years ago, or, perhaps closely related, the expulsion from the Garden of Eden. Or the writing of *Hamlet*, which features a man so anguished, bored, indecisive and generally put-upon by the fact of his own existence that we welcome him into our hearts and find no precursor for him in literature. We can fix the beginnings of the modern mind in the scientific revolution of the seventeenth century; the agricultural or industrial revolutions which gathered populations into cities, and eventually made possible mass consumption, mass political parties, mass communication; with the writings of Kafka, a most artfully or wilfully dissociated sensibility; or with the invention of writing itself, a mere several thousand years ago, which made possible an exponential increase in the transmission of culture; the publication of Einstein's Special and General Theories, the first performance of *The Rite of Spring*, the publication of Joyce's *Ulysses*, or the dropping of a nuclear weapon on Hiroshima, after which we accepted, whether we wanted it or not, stewardship for the entire planet. Some used to plump for the storming of the Winter Palace, though I'd prefer to that the radically unadorned, conversationally reflective early poetry of Wordsworth; or by association, the English or French Enlightenments and the invention of universal human rights.

The biological view, on the other hand, is long and, by these terms, unspectacular, though I would say no less interesting: one speaks not of a moment, but of an immeasurable tract of irretrievable time whose traces are a handful of bones and stone artefacts which demand all our interpretative genius. With the neo-cortex evolving at the astonishing rate of an extra teaspoon of grey matter every hundred-thousand years, hominids made tools, acquired language, became aware of their own existence and that of others, and of their mortality, took a view on the afterlife, and accordingly buried their dead. Possibly the Neanderthals who fell into extinction

30,000 years ago were the first into the modern age. But they just weren't modern enough to survive the pace.

You could say that what is pursued in all these accounts is the secular equivalent of a creation myth. Literary writers seem to prefer an explosive, decisive moment, the miracle of a birth, to a dull continuum of infinitesimal change. More or less the whole timespan of culture can be embraced when we ask, Who is the oldest, who is the *ur*, modern human being: mitochondrial Eve, or Alan Turing?

Our interest in the roots of modernity is not just a consequence of accelerating social change: implicit in the idea of the definitive moment, of rupture with the past, is the notion that human nature is a specific historical product, shaped by shared values, circumstances of upbringing within a certain civilisation – in other words, that there is no human nature at all beyond that which develops at a particular time and in a particular culture. By this view the mind is an all-purpose, infinitely adaptable computing machine operating a handful of wired-in rules. We are born tabula rasa, and it is our times that shape us.

This view, known to some as the Standard Social Science Model, and to others as environmental determinism, was the dominant one in the twentieth century, particularly in its first half. It had its roots in anthropology, especially in the work of Margaret

Mead and her followers, and in behavioural psychology. Writing in *Sex and Temperament in Three Primitive Societies*, published in 1935, Mead wrote: 'We are forced to conclude that human nature is almost unbelievably malleable, responding accurately and contrastingly to contrasting cultural conditions.' This view found endorsement across the social sciences, and solidified in the post-war years into a dogma that had clear political dimensions. There was a time when to challenge it with reference to a biological dimension to existence would be to court academic, and even social, pariah status. Like Christian theologians, the cultural relativists freed us from all biological constraints, and set mankind apart from all other life on earth. And within this view, the educated man or woman pronouncing on a favoured date for the transformation of human nature would be on firm ground epistemologically – we are what the world makes us, and when the world changes dramatically, then so do we in our essentials. It can all happen, as Virginia Woolf observed for herself, 'on or about December 1910'.

The famous behaviourist, John Watson, Professor of Psychology at Johns Hopkins, published an influential book on child-rearing in 1928. As Christina Hardyment showed in her marvellous book, *Dream Babies*, there is hardly a better window into the collective mind of a society, its view of human nature, than the childcare handbooks it produces. Watson wrote:

> Give me a dozen healthy infants, well-formed, and my own specified world to bring them up in and I'll guarantee to take any one at random and train him to become any kind of specialist I might select – doctor, lawyer, merchant chief, and yes, even beggarman and thief, regardless of his talents, penchants, tendencies, abilities, vocations and race of his ancestors.

Human nature was clay in his hands. I can't help feeling that the following passage from Watson's childcare book, *The Psychological Care of Young Infants*, beyond its unintentional comedy, reflects or foretells a century of doomed, tragic social experiments in shaping human nature, and shows us a skewed science, devoid of evidence, and no less grotesque than the pseudo-science that perverted Darwin's work to promote theories of racial supremacy:

> The sensible way to bring up children is to treat them as young adults. Dress them, bathe them with care and circumspection. Let your behaviour always be objective and kindly firm. Never hug and kiss them. Never let them sit in your lap. If you must, kiss them once on the forehead when they say

goodnight. Shake hands with them in the morning. Give them a pat on the head when they make a good job of a difficult task ... Put the child out in the backyard a large part of the time ... Do this from the time that it is born ... Let it learn to overcome difficulties almost from the moment of birth ... away from your watchful eye. If your heart is too tender, and you must watch the child, make yourself a peephole, so that you can see without being seen, or use a periscope.

Watson's book, hugely successful at the time, was pronounced by *Atlantic Monthly* to be 'a godsend to parents'.

The ideas of Mead and Watson, who were simply prominent figures among many promoting the near infinite malleability of human nature, found general acceptance in the public, and in the universities, where their descendants flourish today in various forms. No one should doubt that some good impulses lay behind the Standard Model. Margaret Mead in particular, working at a time when the European empires had consolidated but had not yet begun to crumble, had a strong anti-racist element to her work, and she was determined to oppose the condescending view of primitive inferiority and to insist that each culture must be judged in its own terms. When Mead and Watson were at their most active, the Soviet revolution still held great hopes for mankind. If learning makes us what we are, then inequalities could be eliminated if we shared the same environment. Educate parents in the proper methods of childcare, and new generations of improved people would emerge. Human nature could be fundamentally re-moulded by the makers of social policy. We were perfectible, and the wrongs and inequalities of the past could be rectified by radical alterations to the social environment. The cruelties and absurdities of Social Darwinism and eugenics and, later, the new threat posed by the social policies of Hitler's Germany, engendered a disgust with the biological perspective that helped entrench a belief in a socially determined nature that could be engineered for the better of all.

In fact, the Third Reich cast a long shadow over free scientific enquiry in the decades after the Second World War. Various branches of psychology were trapped by intellectual fear, deterred by recent history from considering the mind as a biological product of adaptive forces, even while, in nearby biology departments, from the 1940s onwards, Darwinism was uniting with Mendelian genetics and molecular biology to form the powerful alliance known as the Modern Synthesis.

In the late fifties, the young Paul Ekman, who had no firm convictions of his own, set off for New Guinea with head-and-shoulder photographs of modern Americans expressing various emotions – surprise, fear, disgust, joy and so on. He discovered that his sample group of Stone Age Highlanders, who had had no, or virtually no, contact with the modern world, were able to make up easily recognisable stories about each expression. They also mimed for him the facial expressions in response to stories he gave them – you come across a pig that has been dead for some days. His work, and later, cleverly designed experiments with Japanese and Americans, which took into account the display rules of the different cultures, clearly vindicated Darwin's conclusions. As Ekman writes:

> Social experience influences attitudes about emotion, creates display and feeling rules, develops and tunes the particular occasions which will most rapidly call forth an emotion. The *expression* of our emotions, the particular configurations of muscular movements, however, appear to be fixed, enabling understanding across generations, across cultures, and within cultures between strangers as well as intimates.

Before leaving for New Guinea he had paid a visit to Margaret Mead. Her firm view was that facial expressions differ from culture to culture as much as customs and values. She was distinctly cool about

Ekman's research. And yet towards the end of her life she explained in her autobiography in 1972 that she and her colleagues had held back from the consideration of the biological bases of behaviour because of anxieties about the political consequences. How strange, this reversal of historical circumstances, that for Mead universality in expression or in human nature should appear to lend support to racism, while for Darwin such considerations undermined its flimsy theoretical basis.

Mead and her generation of anthropologists, arriving at a Stone Age settlement with their notebooks, gifts and decent intentions, did not fully understand (though Darwin, along with most novelists, could have told them), as they exchanged smiles and greetings with their subjects, what a vast pool of shared humanity, of shared assumptions, was necessary, and already being drawn on, for them to do their work. As the last of these precious cultures have vanished, the data was revisited. Donald Brown, in his book *Human Universals* (1991), compiled a list of what human individuals and societies hold in common. It is both long and, given the near infinite range of all possible patterns of behaviour, quite specific. When reading it, it is worth bearing in mind Wilson's termite dean. Brown includes – I'm choosing at random – tool making, preponderant right-handedness, specific childhood fears, knowledge that other people have an inner life, trade, giving of gifts, notions of justice, importance of gossip, hospitality, hierarchies and so on. What's interesting about Brown's characterisation of what he calls the 'Universal People', who incorporate all the common, shared features of mankind, is the number of pages he devotes to language – again quite specific. For example, Universal People language has contrasts between vowels and contrasts between stops and non-stops. Their language is symbolic, invariably contains nouns, verbs and the possessive. Extra proficiency in language invariably confers prestige. This, surely, at the higher level of mental functioning, is what binds the human family. We know now that no blank-disk all-purpose machine could learn language at the speed and facility that a child does. A three-year-old daily solves scores of ill-posed problems. An instinct for language is a central part of our nature.

On our crowded planet, we are no longer able to visit Stone Age peoples untouched by modern times. Mead and her contemporaries would never have wanted to put the question, What is it that we hold in common with such people? and anthropologists no longer have the opportunity of first contact. We can, however, reach to our bookshelves. Literature must be our anthropology. Here is a description – 2,700 years old – of a woman who has been waiting for more than two decades for her beloved husband to come home. Someone has told her that he has at last arrived, and is downstairs, and that she must go and greet him. But, she asks herself, is it really him?

> *She started down from her lofty room, her heart*
> *in turmoil, torn . . . should she keep her distance,*
> *probe her husband? Or rush up to the man at once*
> *and kiss his head and cling to both his hands?*
> *As soon as she stepped over the stone threshold,*
> *slipping in, she took a seat at the closest wall*
> *and, radiant in the firelight, faced Odysseus now.*
> *There he sat, leaning against the great central column,*
> *eyes fixed on the ground, waiting, poised for whatever*
> > *words*
> *his hardy wife might say when she caught sight of him.*
> *A long while she sat in silence . . . numbing wonder*
> *filled her heart as her eyes explored his face.*
> *One moment he seemed . . . Odysseus to the man,*
> > *to the life –*
> *the next, no, he was not the man she knew,*
> *a huddled mass of rags was all she saw.*

So, still uncertain, Penelope tells Odysseus they'll sleep in separate rooms, and she gives orders for the marriage bed to be moved out of the bedroom. But of course, he knows this bed can't be moved – he knocked it together himself, and reminds her just how he did it. Thus he proves beyond doubt he really is her husband; but now he's upset that she thought he was an imposter, and they're already heading for a marital spat.

> *Penelope felt her knees go slack, her heart surrender,*
> *recognising the strong clear signs that Odysseus offered.*
> *She dissolved in tears, rushed to Odysseus, flung*
> > *her arms*
> *around his neck and kissed his head and cried out,*
> *'Odysseus – don't flare up at me now, not you,*
> *always the most understanding man alive!*
> *The gods, it was the gods who sent us sorrow –*
> *they grudged us both a life in each other's arms*
> *from the heady zest of youth to the stoop of old age.*
> *But don't fault me, angry with me now because I failed,*
> *at the first glimpse, to greet you, hold you, so . . .*
> *In my heart of hearts I always cringed with fear*
> *some fraud might come, beguile me with his talk.*

Customs may change – dead suitors may be lying in the hallway, with no homicide charges pending – but we recognise the human essence of these lines. Within the emotional and the expressive we remain what we are. As Darwin put it in his conclusion to the *Expression*, 'the language of the emotions . . . is certainly of importance for the welfare of mankind'. In Homer's case we extend Ekman's 'understanding across the generations' – a hundred and thirty of them at least.

THE HUMAN GENOME Sequencing Consortium concluded a report in *Nature* in 2001 with these words: 'Finally, it has not escaped our notice that the more we learn about the human genome, the more there is to explore.' This form of respectful echoing within the tradition should appeal to those who admire literary modernism. When the sequencing of the human genome was completed, it was reasonable to ask whose genome this was anyway? What lucky individual had been chosen to represent us all? Who is the universal person? The answer was that the genes of fifteen people were merged into just the sort of composite, plausible, imaginary person a novelist might dream up, and here we contemplate the metaphorical convergence of these two noble and distinct forms of investigation into our condition, literature and science. That which binds us, our common nature, is what literature has always, knowingly and helplessly, given voice to. And it is this universality which the biological sciences, entering another exhilarating phase, are set to explore further.

Hilary Lecture, Oxford, 2003

2

The Originality of the Species

IN JUNE 1858 a slender package from Ternate, an island off the Dutch East Indies, arrived for Charles Darwin at his country home in Downe, Kent. He may well have recognised the handwriting as that of Alfred Wallace, with whom he had been in correspondence and from whom he was hoping to receive some specimens. But what Darwin found in the package along with a covering letter was a short essay. And this essay was to transform Darwin's life.

Wallace's twenty pages, so it seemed to their reader on that momentous morning, covered all the principal ideas of evolution by natural selection that Darwin had been working on for more than two decades and which he thought were his exclusive possession – and which he had yet to publish. Wallace, working alone, with very little in the way of encouragement or money, drew from his extensive experience of natural history, gathered while sending back specimens for collectors. He articulated concisely the elements as well as the sources familiar to Darwin: artificial selection, the struggle for survival, competition and extinction, the way species changed into different forms by an impersonal, describable process, by a logic that did not need the intervention of a deity. Wallace, like Darwin, had been influenced by the geological speculations of Charles Lyell, and the population theories of Thomas Malthus.

In a covering letter Wallace politely asked Darwin to forward the essay to Lyell. Now, Darwin could have quietly destroyed Wallace's package and no one would have known a thing – it had taken months to arrive, and the mail between the Dutch East Indies could hardly have been reliable in the mid-nineteeth century. But Darwin was an honourable man, and knew that he could never live with himself if he behaved scurrilously. And yet he was in anguish. In his own letter to Lyell that accompanied Wallace's essay, which Darwin forwarded the same day, he lamented: 'So all my originality, whatever it may amount to, will be smashed.' He was surprised at the depth of his own feelings about priority, about being first. As Janet Browne notes in her biography of Darwin, the excitement of discovery in his work had been replaced by profound anxieties about possession and ownership. He was ambushed by low emotions – mortification, irritation, rancour. In a much-quoted phrase, he was 'full of trumpery feelings'.

He had held off publishing his own work in a desire to perfect it, to amass instances, to make it as immune to disproof as he could. And, of course, he was aware of his work's theological implications – and that had made him cautious too. But he had been 'forestalled'. That day he decided he must yield priority to Wallace. He must, he wrote, 'resign myself to my fate'.

Within a day he had even more pressing concerns. His fifteen-year-old daughter, Henrietta, fell ill and there was fear that she had diphtheria. The next day the baby, Charles, his and Emma's tenth and last child, developed a fever. Soon, Lyell was urging Darwin to concede nothing and to publish a 'sketch', which would conclusively prove Darwin's priority over Wallace.

Taking his turn to nurse the sick baby, Darwin could decide nothing, and left the matter to his close friend Joseph Hooker, and to Lyell. They discussed the matter and proposed that Darwin's 'sketch' should be read aloud along with Wallace's essay at a meeting of the Linnaean Society, and the two pieces would be published in the society's journal. Speed was important. Wallace might have sent his essay to a magazine, in which case Darwin's priority would be sunk, or at least compromised. There was no time to ask Wallace's permission to have his essay read.

But before Darwin could consider the proposal, the baby died. In his grief, Darwin hastily made a compilation for Hooker to edit. An 1844 set of notes, though out of date, seemed to make a conclusive case for priority, for they bore Hooker's pencilled marks. A more recent 1857 letter to Asa Grey, the professor of botany at Harvard, set out concisely Darwin's thoughts on evolution by natural selection.

Lyell, Hooker and Darwin were eminent insiders in the closed world of Victorian metropolitan science. Wallace was the outsider. He came from a far humbler background, and if he was known at all, it was as a provider of material for gentlemen experts. It was customary at the Linnaean Society for double contributions to be read in alphabetical order. And so, in Darwin's absence – he and Emma buried their baby that day – his 1844 notes were followed by his detailed 1857 letter, and then, almost as a footnote, came Wallace's 1858 essay.

DARWIN HAD DELVED far deeper over many years and certainly deserved priority. Wallace found it difficult to think through the implications of natural selection, and was reluctant in later years to allow that humans too were subject to evolutionary change.

The point, however, is Darwin's mortification about losing possession. As he wrote later to Hooker, 'I always thought it very possible that I might be forestalled, but I fancied that I had a grand enough soul not to care.'

Hooker began to press his friend to write a proper scientific paper on natural selection. Darwin protested. He needed to set out all the facts, and they could not be accommodated within a single paper. Hooker persisted, and so Darwin began his essay, which in time grew to become *On the Origin of Species*. In Browne's description, it suddenly released 'years of pent-up caution'. Back at Downe House, Darwin did not use a desk, but sat in an armchair with a board across his knees and wrote like a fiend. 'All the years of thought', writes Browne, 'climaxed in these months of final insight ... the fire within came from Wallace.'

The *Origin*, written in thirteen months, represents an extraordinary intellectual feat: mature insight, deep knowledge and observational powers, the marshalling of facts, the elucidation of near-irrefutable arguments in the service of a profound insight into natural processes. The reluctance to upset his wife Emma's religious devotion, or to contradict the theological certainties of his scientific colleagues, or to find himself in the unlikely role of iconoclast, a radical dissenter in Victorian society – all were swept aside for fear of another man taking possession of and getting credit for the ideas he believed to be his.

IN MODERN TIMES, we have come to take for granted in art – literature as well as painting and cinema – the vital and enduring concept of originality. Despite all kinds of theoretical objections, it remains central to our notion of quality. It carries with it an idea of the *new*, of something created in a godlike fashion out of nothing. 'Perfectly unborrowed', as Coleridge said of Wordsworth's poetry. Originality is inseparable from a powerful sense of the individual, and the boundaries of this individuality are strongly protected.

In traditional societies, conformity to certain respected patterns and conventions was the norm. The pot, the carving, the exquisite weaving needed no signature. By contrast, the modern artefact bears the stamp of personality. The work *is* the signature. The individual truly possesses his or her own work, has rights in it, and is defined by it. It is private property that cannot be trespassed on. A great body of law has grown up around this possessiveness. Countries that do not sign up to the Berne Convention and other international agreements relating to intellectual property rights find themselves excluded from the mainstream of a globalised culture. The artist owns her work, and sits glowering over it, like a broody hen on her eggs. We see the intensity of this fusion of originality and individuality whenever a plagiarism scandal erupts.

The dust-jacket photograph, though barely relevant to an appreciation of a novel, seals the ownership. This is me, it says, and what you have in your hands is mine. Or is me. We see it too in the cult of personality that surrounds the artist – individuality and personality are driven to inspire near-religious devotion. The coach parties at Grasmere, the cult of Hemingway or Picasso or Neruda. These are big figures – their lives fascinate us sometimes more than their art.

This fascination is relatively new. In their day, Shakespeare, Bach, Mozart, even Beethoven were not worshipped, they did not gleam in the social rankings the way their patrons did, or in the way that Byron or Chopin would do, or in the way a Nobel Prize-winner does today. How the humble artist was promoted to the role of secular priest is a large and contentious subject, a sub-chapter in a long speculation about individuality and modernity. The possible causes make a familiar list – capitalism, a growing leisured class, the Protestant faith, the Romantic movement, new technologies of communication, the elaboration of patent law following the Industrial Revolution. Some or all of these have brought us to the point at which the identification of the individual and her creativity is now complete and automatic and unquestionable. The novelist today who signs her name in her book for a reader, and the reader who stands in line waiting for his book to be signed, collude in this marriage of selfhood and art.

There is an antithetical notion of artistic creation, and though it has been expressed in different forms by artists, critics and theoreticians, it has never taken hold outside the academies. This view holds that, of course, no one escapes history. Something cannot come out of nothing, and even a genius is bound by the constraints and opportunities of circumstance. The artist is merely the instrument on which history and culture play. Whether an artist works within his tradition or against it, he remains its helpless product. The title of Auden's essay 'The Dyer's Hand' is just a mild expression of the drift. Techniques and conventions developed by predecessors, perspective, say, or free indirect style (the third-person narrative coloured by a character's subjective state) are available as ready-made tools and have a profound effect. Above all, art is a conversation conducted down through the generations. Meaningful echoes, parody, quotation, rebellion, tribute and pastiche all have their place. Culture, not the individual talent, is the predominant force; in creative-writing classes, young writers are told that if they do not read widely, they are more likely to be helplessly influenced by those whose work they do not know.

SUCH A VIEW of cultural inheritance is naturally friendly to science. Darwin worked against a background of all kinds of evolutionary views, including those of his grandfather, Erasmus. Darwin relied on the observations of animal breeders, pigeon fanciers, natural historians, as well as the work of Malthus and Lyell. Einstein, another great creator, could not have begun his Special Theory of Relativity without the benefit of countless others, including Hendrik Lorentz and Max Planck. He was entirely dependent on mathematicians to give expression to his ideas. (Newton's much-cited claim to have stood on the shoulders of giants was inverted some years ago to illustrate the potency of predecessors in science: 'If I have seen less far than others, it was because giants were standing on my shoulders.')

Given the tools that were available to scientists in the mid-twentieth century, including X-ray crystallography, and given the suppositions that were in the air, and the different groups that were working in this field, DNA would have been described sooner or later by someone or other. It should hardly matter then, in the realms of pure rationality and scientific advance, who actually got there first. If it had been Linus Pauling and not Crick and Watson, what difference would it have made in the sum of things? But what a difference being ahead by a few months made to the lives of Crick and Watson.

In terms of the general good, can it matter whether Joseph Priestley or Antoine Lavoisier discovered oxygen, or whether Isaac Newton or Gottfried Leibniz devised the calculus?

Consider another celebrated moment of priority-anxiety. It came at the end of a ten-year process during which Einstein pursued the ambitious project of 'generalising' his Special Theory of Relativity, formulated in 1905. As his thinking developed in the years after its publication, he predicted that light would be influenced by gravitation. His biographer Walter Isaacson points out that Einstein's success thus far had 'been based on his special talent for sniffing out the underlying physical principles of nature', leaving to others the more mundane task of providing the best mathematical expression. 'But', as Isaacson notes, 'by 1912 Einstein had come to appreciate that maths could be a tool for discovering – and not merely describing – nature's laws.'

Isaacson quotes the physicist James Hartle: 'The central idea of general relativity is that gravity arises from the curvature of space-time.' Two complementary processes were to be described: how matter is affected by a gravitational field, and how matter generates a gravitational field in space-time and causes it to curve. These startling, near-ungraspable notions were eventually to find expression in Einstein's adaptation of the non-Euclidean geometry of tensors devised by the mathematicians Riemann and Ricci. By 1912 Einstein had come close to a mathematical strategy for an equation, but then he turned aside, looking for a more physics-based route. It was only partially successful, and he had to be satisfied with publishing with his colleague Marcel Grossmann an outline of a theory, the famous '*Entwurf*' of 1913, which, as Einstein came to realise, contained important errors.

The upheavals of the First World War, and Einstein's struggle against German nationalism among scientific colleagues, his ongoing attempts to see his young sons in Zurich and to obtain a divorce from their mother form the background to another extraordinary intellectual supernova, extending not over thirteen months this time, but four outstanding weeks.

In June of 1915 Einstein lectured on the *Entwurf* at the University of Göttingen. The lectures were a great success. Also, in private conversations with the eminent German mathematician David Hilbert, a fellow pacifist, Einstein explained relativity and what he was attempting, and the mathematical problems he was encountering. Afterwards, Einstein declared himself enchanted with Hilbert. He seemed to understand right down to the fine details what Einstein was trying to achieve, and the mathematical obstacles in his way.

In fact, Hilbert understood rather too well, and soon he was working hard to find a formulation of his own for a general theory, just as Einstein was discovering more errors and contradictions in the *Entwurf*. He abandoned it in October and turned back to the maths-based strategy of 1912. And thus, painfully conscious of Hilbert, the superior mathematician, on his heels, Einstein began what Isaacson, surely rightly, calls 'the most concentrated frenzies of scientific creativity in history'. As he worked on his theory, he was presenting his ideas immediately to the Prussian Academy in a set of four weekly lectures, beginning on 4 November 1915.

By his third lecture, Einstein's theory in its present state accurately predicted the shift in Mercury's orbit – he was, he wrote to a friend, 'beside myself with joyous excitement'. Just days before Einstein was about to give his final lecture, Hilbert submitted his own formulation of general relativity to a journal in an essay with the not so humble title of 'The Foundation of Physics'. Einstein wrote bitterly to a friend: 'In my personal experience I have hardly come to know the wretchedness of mankind better.'

Unlike Wallace, who worked independently of Darwin, Hilbert was trying to give mathematical expression to theories that were Einstein's. Nevertheless, Einstein, like Darwin, was driven to a great creative outpouring for fear of losing priority. The formulation he gave in his final lecture on 28 November was described by the physicist Max Born as 'the greatest feat of human thinking about nature, the most amazing combination of philosophical penetration, physical intuition and mathematical skill'. Einstein himself said of the theory that it was of 'incomparable beauty'.

The Einstein-Hilbert priority dispute still rumbles on in its small way. But it should be noted that both Wallace and Hilbert were quick and generous to concede priority to Darwin and Einstein. If Einstein's friendship with Hilbert became strained during that momentous month of November 1915, their friendship was soon re-established.

AS CHILDREN WE race each other to be first into the sea. There have been heroic, sometimes fatal races to be first at the North or South Poles, or round the North-West Passage or up this river or across that desert. Sometimes, intense nationalistic passions are involved. First to swim or fly across the Channel, first to ascend into space, first on the Moon, on Mars – these great endeavours, for all their heroism and technical accomplishment, have a childlike quality.

In literature, everyone is first. We do not need to ask who was first to write *Don Quixote*. Better, in fact, to consider the possibility of being the second, like Pierre Menard, who in Borges's famous story independently reconceives, centuries after Cervantes, the entire novel, down to the last word. The worst novelist in the world can at least be assured that he will be the first to write his terrible novel. And, mercifully, the last. And yet, to be first, to originate, to be original, is key to the quality of a work of literature. However minimally, it must advance – in subject matter, in means of expression – our understanding of ourselves, of ourselves in the world.

But novelists are the grateful inheritors of an array of techniques and conventions and subject matter, which themselves are the products of social change. I've mentioned free indirect style, first deployed in extended form by Jane Austen. Samuel Richardson's novel *Clarissa* was perhaps the first to describe in exacting detail and at length the qualities of a subjective mental state. Nineteenth-century novelists bequeathed penetrating and sophisticated means for delineating character. A long time had to pass before a novelist troubled to inhabit the mind of a child. In *Ulysses*, Joyce made a new poetry out of the minutiae of the everyday. And he and modernists like Virginia Woolf found new means of representing the flow of consciousness that now are common, even in children's books. But Richardson, Austen, Joyce and Woolf were inheritors in their turn. They sat on the shoulders of giants too.

Darwin and Einstein came first and were overwhelmed by celebrity and profound respect, and became icons in the culture, while Wallace and Hilbert languished in relative obscurity. And this 'first', this originality, is precisely defined. Not first along an absolute Newtonian timeline, but first in a recognisable and respectable public forum. Hence the Linnaean Society, hence the Prussian Academy – presentations made at speed and under immense pressure.

Nineteenth-century science had teetered for decades on the edge of evolutionary ideas, and if Darwin – or for that matter Wallace – had not given expression to the idea of evolution by natural selection, others surely would have. The same biological realities confronted everyone, and taxonomy was at an advanced stage.

Likewise, it is inconceivable that the brilliant generation that laid down the foundations of classical quantum mechanics in the first thirty years of the twentieth century would not have found a means of binding matter, energy, space and time, though their routes may have differed from Einstein's, and they may not at first have achieved it with such elegant economy by way of Riemann's tensor.

To be first, to be original in science, matters profoundly. Laboratories race each other to publication. Powerful passions are involved, and Nobel prizes too. To be for ever associated with a certain successful idea is a form of immortality. In longing for it, scientists demonstrate a concern for themselves as creators, as irreplaceable makers. In this we see a parallel with the fiercely individualistic world of novelists, poets, artists and composers who know in their hearts that they are utterly reliant on those who went before them. In both, we see a human face.

I WANT TO touch on another point of convergence between the arts and science. And this is the question of aesthetics. In 1858 and 1915, Darwin and Einstein, driven in part by the somewhat ignoble or worldly ambition to be first, redirected not only the course of science, but redefined our sense of ourselves. These twin revolutions, barely sixty years apart, represent the most profound as well as the most rapid shift and dislocation in human thought that has ever occurred. This rapidity is worth considering. The counter-intuitive notion that the Earth revolves around the Sun took generations to spread and take hold across Europe. Likewise, the brilliant invention of three- and four-crop rotation. A teeming microscopic world was available to medicine from the time in the 1670s onwards when Antoni van

Leeuwenhoek began sending his observations to the Royal Society in London. But stubborn tradition-bound medicine kept its back turned on science, and it took almost another 200 years before an understanding of harmful microorganisms and the concept of anti-sepsis shaped medical practice.

A theory that suggested the relatedness of all species, including humans, was a challenge to dignity, and the church found it hard at first to accept the suggestion that species were not fixed, unchanging and recently made by God. Generally, however, Darwin's ideas explained too much, too well, and were too much in accord with new observations in geology to be resisted, especially by biologists, and many English clergymen with country livings were good naturalists and could immediately grasp the theory's utility. What is interesting about the publication of *On the Origin of Species* is the rapidity of its acceptance.

Einstein's theory could be empirically tested by observing the degree of refraction of starlight by the Sun, best achieved at a full eclipse. Various expeditions were sent from 1918, and though they returned what seemed a positive result, in reality the margin of error in measurements was too great to provide absolute confirmation. And, meanwhile, the theory was already in the textbooks by the late 1920s. Radio telescopes in the early 1950s provided the definitive proof, and by then relativity theory was a staple of physics and astronomy.

The accelerated acceptance of Darwin and Einstein's work from 1859 and 1916 cannot be explained entirely by reference to their effectiveness or truthfulness. Here is what the great American biologist E. O. Wilson has to say about a scientific theory: 'The elegance, we can fairly say the beauty, of any particular scientific generalisation is measured by its simplicity relative to the number of phenomena it can explain.' Many physicists, notably Steven Weinberg, are convinced that it was the elegance, the sheer beauty, of Einstein's general theory that drove its rapid acceptance ahead of its empirical validation.

Those lucky enough to understand Paul Dirac's famous equation (it explains the spin of the electron and predicted the existence of anti-matter) speak of its intellectual daring and breathtaking beauty. This is a music most of us will never hear. The equation, as brief as Einstein's, can be found carved in stone in Westminster Abbey.

If one might make use of Darwin's theory to think about Einstein's, we could speculate that evolution has granted us only sufficient understanding of space and time as is necessary to function and reproduce effectively. The relentless logic of natural selection is not organised to grant organisms, even most humans, an intuitive grasp of the kinds of counter-intuitive insights that the special and general theories of Einstein present.

Gravity may well be a function of the bending of space-time, matter and energy may lie along a continuum, but most of us cannot feel this as part of our immediate world. We are the evolved inhabitants of Middle Earth. You might say we continue to dwell in a Newtonian universe, but in fact it is one that would also be familiar to Jesus and Plato.

When a well-known scientist, John Wheeler, writes that 'matter tells space-time how to curve, and curved space-time tells matter how to move', we may or may not be impressed, but it is hard to reorient one's worldview accordingly, to abandon the sense that there is an absolute 'now' in every corner of the universe and that empty space is just a void ready to be filled, and cannot be bent, and is a distinct entity from time. The Einsteinian revolution may have redefined the absolute basics of matter, energy, space and time, but the limits of our mental equipment keep us in our evolutionary homelands, in the savannah of common sense.

On the other hand, as Steven Pinker has pointed out, the ramifications of natural selection are multiple. And, relatively, they are easily, if uneasily, understood: the Earth and life on it are far older than the Bible suggests. Species are not fixed entities created at one time. They rise, fall, become extinct, and there is no purpose, no forethought in these patterns. We can explain these processes now without reference to the supernatural. We ourselves are related, however distantly, to all living things. We can explain our *own* existence without reference to the supernatural. We may have no purpose at all except to continue. We have a nature derived in part from our evolutionary past. Underlying natural selection are physical laws. The evolved material entity we call the brain is what makes consciousness possible. When it is damaged, so is mental function. There is no evidence for an immortal soul, and no good reason beyond fervent hope that consciousness survives the death of the brain.

It is testimony to the originality as well as the diversity of our species that some of us find such ramifications horrifying, or irritating, or self-evidently untrue and (literally) soulless, while others find them both beautiful and liberating and discover, with Darwin, 'grandeur in this view of life'. Either way, if we do not find our moments of exaltation in religious awe and the contemplation of a supreme supernatural being, we will find them in the contemplation of our arts and our science. When Einstein found that his general theory made correct predictions for the shift in Mercury's orbit, he felt so thrilled he had palpitations, 'as if something had snapped inside. I was,' he wrote, 'beside myself with joyous excitement.' This is the excitement any artist can recognise. This is the joy, not of simple description, but of creation. It is the expression, common to both the arts and science, of the somewhat grand, somewhat ignoble, all-too-human pursuit of originality in the face of total dependence on the achievements of others.

Darwin Symposium, Santiago, Chile, 2009

3

A Parallel Tradition

THOSE WHO LOVE literature rather take for granted the idea of a literary tradition. In part, it is a temporal map, a means of negotiating the centuries and the connections between writers. It helps to know that Shakespeare preceded Keats who preceded Wilfred Owen, because lines of influence might be traced. And in part, a tradition implies a hierarchy, a canon; conventionally, it has Shakespeare dominant, like a lonely figurine on top of a wedding cake, and all the other writers arranged on descending tiers. In recent years the cake has seemed to many too inedibly male and middle-class and heterosexual. What remains undisputed is the value of the canon itself. To define a tradition is to make an argument and expect to be engaged.

Above all, a literary tradition implies an active

historical sense of a past, that lives in and shapes the present. Reciprocally, a work of literature produced now, infinitesimally shifts our understanding of what has gone before. You cannot value a poet alone, T. S. Eliot argued in 'Tradition and the Individual Talent', 'you must set him, for contrast and comparison, among the dead'. Eliot did not find it preposterous 'that the past should be altered by the present as much as the present is directed by the past'. We might discern the ghost of Jane Austen in a novel by Angus Wilson, or hear echoes of Wordsworth in a poem by Alice Oswald. Ideally, having read our contemporaries, we return to re-read the dead poets with a fresh understanding. In a living artistic tradition, the dead never lie down.

Can science and science writing, a vast and half-forgotten accumulation over the centuries, offer us a parallel living tradition? If it can, how do we begin to describe it? The problems of choice are equalled only by those of criteria. Literature does not improve; it changes. Science, on the other hand, as an intricate, self-correcting thought system, advances and refines its understanding of thousands of fields of study. This is how it derives its power and status. Science prefers to forget much of its past. It is constitutionally bound to a form of selective amnesia.

Is accuracy, being on the right track, or some approximation of it, the most important criterion for selection? Or is style the final arbiter? The writings of Thomas Browne or Francis Bacon or Robert Burton contain many fine passages that we now know to be factually wrong – but we would surely not wish to exclude them. The tradition must keep a place for Aristotle and Galen because of the hold they had over people's minds for centuries. We have to beware of implying a Whig history of science, a history of the lonely but correct road that leads to the present. We need to remember the various discarded toys of science – the humours, the four elements, phlogiston, the ether and, more recently, protoplasm. Modern chemistry was born out of the futile ambitions of alchemy. Scientists who hurl themselves down blind alleys perform a service – they save everyone a great deal of trouble. They may also refine techniques along the way, and offer points of resistance, intellectual cantilevers, to their contemporaries.

I say all this somewhat dutifully, because there actually is a special pleasure to be shared when a scientist or science writer leads us towards the light of a powerful idea which in turn opens avenues of exploration and discovery leading far into the future, binding many different phenomena in many different fields of study. Some might call this truth. It has an aesthetic value that is not to be found in Galen's confident and muddled assertions about the nature of disease. For example, there is something of the luminous quality of great literature when the twenty-nine-year-old Charles Darwin, just two years back from his *Beagle* voyage and twenty-one years before he will publish *On the Origin of Species*, confides to a pocket notebook the first hints of a simple, beautiful idea: 'Origin of man now proved . . . He who understands baboon would do more towards metaphysics than Locke.'

Far better, perhaps, to set aside issues of truth and inaccuracy, criteria and definitions. We know what we like when we taste it. Until recently, the purely literary tradition was never obliged to set out its terms. The work came first, and then the talk about it. In a sense, I am merely making an appeal for a grand parlour game: what might a scientific literary tradition be? Which books are going on our shelves? To propose is to ask to be challenged; already I suspect my own suggestions are too male, too middle-class, too Eurocentric.

Here is the opening of an essay – strictly speaking, a letter – on immunology.

> It is whispered in Christian Europe that the English are mad and maniacs: mad because they give their children smallpox to prevent their getting it, and maniacs because they cheerfully communicate to their children a certain and terrible illness with the object of preventing an uncertain one. The English

> on their side say: 'The other Europeans are cowardly and unnatural: cowardly in that they are afraid of giving a little pain to their children, and unnatural because they expose them to death from smallpox some time in the future.' To judge who is right in this dispute, here is the history of this famous inoculation which is spoken of with such horror outside England.

This is Voltaire, writing in the late 1720s during an extended visit to England, presenting a rare instance of a French intellectual impressed by English ideas. Voltaire wrote beautifully in his *Lettres philosophiques* – translated as *Letters on England* – on religion, politics and literature. He was delighted by the degree of political freedom he found here, by the powers of Parliament, the absence of religious absolutism and divine right. He attended Newton's funeral and was amazed that a humble scientist was buried like a king in Westminster Abbey. Crucially, he placed himself between a scientist and an interested public, and offered superb expositions of Newton's theories of optics and gravitation which still stand today. If you want to know what was daring and original in what Newton said, read Voltaire. He communicates the excitement of a new idea, and sets the highest standards of lucidity.

In 2001, when my son William came to study

biology at UCL he was advised to read no papers on genetics written before 1997. By 2003, estimates of the human genome had shrunk by a factor of five, or even six. Such is the headlong nature of contemporary science. But if we understand science merely as a band of light moving through time, advancing on the darkness, and leaving ignorant darkness behind it, always at its best only in the incandescent present, we turn our backs on an epic tale of ingenuity and heroic curiosity.

Here is a man who has polished a lens with infinite care. He has taken some water from a lake and has been studying it scrupulously, with an open mind:

> I found floating therein divers earthy particles and some green streaks, spirally wound serpent-wise and orderly arranged ... Other particles had but the beginning of the foresaid streak; but all consisted of very small green globules joined together; and there were very many small green globules as well ... These animalcules had divers colours, some being whitish and transparent, others with green and very glittering little scales ... And the motion of most of these animalcules in the water was so swift, and so various upwards, downwards and roundabout, that 'twas wonderful to see: and I judge that some of these little creatures were above a thousand times smaller than the smallest ones I have ever yet seen ...

This is Anton van Leeuwenhoek writing from Holland to the Royal Society in 1674, giving the first account of spirogyra, among other organisms. He sent his observations to the Royal Society over a period of fifty years, and it was no accident that he should have sent his letters there. At that time, in a small space, within a triangle formed by London, Cambridge and Oxford, and within a couple of generations, there existed nearly all the world's science. Newton, Locke, Hume (I think we need to include certain philosophers), Willis, Hooke, Boyle, Wren, Flamsteed, Halley: an incredible concentration of talent, and the core of our library – its classical moment.

I have never been persuaded by the common argument that religion and science inhabit different realms and are therefore not in conflict. That the dead inhabit an afterlife, that God exists and made the universe, that prayers are sympathetically heard, that the wicked are punished and the virtuous rewarded are statements about the world in which science takes a deep interest. When Christianity's hold on the world was total, free-thinking Greek and Roman writers of antiquity were largely lost to Medieval science (though not to scholarship in the Islamic lands). Lucretius's long-buried *De Rerum Natura*, rediscovered and highly influential in the early Renaissance, deserves a special place in the literary tradition of science. From the sixteenth century onwards, it was slowly becoming clear that the Church had nothing much useful to say about cosmology, the curing of disease, the age of the earth, the origin of species or any other aspect of the material world. Here is a great scientist, often referred to as 'the father of physics' who has been found 'vehemently suspect of heresy' for promoting the idea that the earth is not at the centre of the solar system and moves around the sun. Under threat of torture by the Inquisition, he was forced to recant. He spent the rest of his days under house arrest.

> having before my eyes and touching with my hands the Holy Gospels, swear that I have always believed, do believe, and with God's help will in the future believe all that is held, preached and taught by the Holy Catholic and Apostolic Church . . . I must altogether abandon the false opinion that the sun is the centre of the world and immovable, and that the earth is not the centre of the world and moves and that I must not hold, defend or teach in any way whatsoever, verbally and in writing the said false doctrine . . .

In 1632 Galileo might or might not have whispered to himself as he signed, 'E pur si muove' (And yet it moves). We will never know. In effect, he pretended to agree that two plus two equals five. To summon

Orwell here is to remember that secular powers have also been hostile to free enquiry. Under Nazi and Soviet regimes science was grotesquely distorted for political ends. The Third Reich's perversion of Darwinian natural selection in the cause of a theory of racial superiority laid the ground for the Holocaust.

Being an earth-bound institution, science itself can hardly claim to be a purely objective pursuit. The canon is rich in human interest, with a history littered with aggressive competition, disputes over priority, accusations of intellectual theft and clashes of powerful personalities. James Watson's *The Double Helix*, published in 1968, is one of the great science books of the twentieth century. But its account of the first accurate description of the structure of DNA is highly personal. Watson's collaborators, Francis Crick and Maurice Wilkins (Rosalind Franklin was dead by this time) took strong exception to the book.

The Double Helix and, eight years later, Richard Dawkins's *The Selfish Gene* marked the beginnings of the golden age of science writing in our time. Dawkins drew on the work of a handful of scientists to make a creative synthesis of Darwinian natural selection and contemporary genetics that excited and delighted even those few who were already familiar with the concepts. It hastened a sea change in evolutionary theory, it affected profoundly the teaching of biology, it enticed an enthusiastic younger generation into the subject and spawned a huge literature.

An important contribution to the development of a living past in science writing was John Carey's *Faber Book of Science*, a magisterial anthology, superbly annotated. In it is the Galileo 'confession' I've just cited. Carey includes a long extract from Thomas Huxley's famous lecture, 'On a Piece of Chalk' to a packed hall of working men in Norwich in 1868. The talk contained the seductive sentence, 'A great chapter in the history of the world is written in the chalk . . .'

Huxley leads us back, of course, to Darwin. The 'Origin' apart, my favourite is *The Expression of the Emotions in Man and Animals* in which he made the case for emotions as human universals shared across cultures. He also made an anti-racist argument for a common human nature. This was one of the first science books to make use of photographs – in this case, one of Darwin's babies bawling in a high chair. The edition by Paul Ekman is an unsurpassed work of scholarship. With a clear sense of a literary tradition, the physicist, Steven Weinberg, in his book *Dreams of a Final Theory*, revisited Huxley's lecture on chalk in the light of contemporary theoretical physics to make an eloquent case for reductionism.

Steven Pinker's application of Darwinian thought to Chomskyan linguistics in *The Language Instinct* is one of the finest celebrations of language I know. Among many other indispensable 'classics', I would propose E. O. Wilson's *The Diversity of Life* on the ecological wonders of the Amazon rainforest, and on the teeming micro-organisms in a handful of soil; David Deutsch's masterly account of the Many Worlds theory in *The Fabric of Reality*; Jared Diamond's melding of history with biological thought in *Guns, Germs and Steel*; Antonio Damasio's hypnotic account of the neuroscience of the emotions in *The Feeling of What Happens*; Matt Ridley, unweaving the opposition of nature and nurture in *Nature via Nurture*; and recently, the philosopher Daniel C. Dennett, conscious of Hume as well as Dawkins, laying out for us the memetics of faith in *Breaking the Spell*.

From Aristotle's empirical study of the marine biology of the Pyrrha lagoon on the island of Lesbos around 344 BC, through to Banks, Faraday, Tyndal, Gauss, Cajal, Einstein, Heisenberg – the scientific literary tradition is vast, rich and multi-lingual. It is a literature that should belong to us all, not just to those who practice science. This is a history of intellectual courage, hard work, occasional inspiration and every conceivable form of human failing. It is also an extended invitation to wonder, to pleasure. Just as we might sit around the kitchen table with friends and celebrate a TV programme, a song, a movie without being actors, composers or directors, so we should be able to make the scientific tradition 'ours' and enjoy this feast of organised curiosity, this sublime achievement of accumulated creativity.

Adapted from a Guardian *article, 2006*

4

End of the World Blues

SINCE 1839, THE world inventory of photographs has been accumulating at an accelerating pace, multiplying into a near infinitude of images, into a resemblance of a Borgesian library. This haunting technology has been with us long enough now that we are able to look at a crowd scene, a busy street, say, in the late-nineteenth century and know for certain that every single figure is dead. Not only the young couple pausing by a park railing, but the child with a hoop and stick, the starchy nurse, the solemn baby upright in its carriage – their lives have run their course, and they are all gone. And yet, frozen in sepia, they appear curiously, busily, oblivious of the fact that they must die – as Susan Sontag put it, 'photographs state the innocence, the vulnerability

of lives heading towards their own destruction.'
'Photography,' she said,

> is the inventory of mortality. A touch of the finger now suffices to invest a moment with posthumous irony. Photographs show people being so irrefutably *there* and at a specific age in their lives; [they] group together people and things which a moment later have already disbanded, changed, continued along the course of their independent destinies.

So, one day, it could be the case with a photograph of us all assembled here today in this hall. Imagine us scrutinised in an old photograph two hundred years hence, idly considered by a future beholder as quaintly old-fashioned, possessed by the self-evident importance of our concerns, ignorant of the date and manner of our certain fate, and long gone. And long gone, en masse.

We are well used to reflections on individual mortality – it is the shaping force in the narrative of our existence. It emerges in childhood as a baffling fact, re-emerges possibly in adolescence as a tragic reality which all around us appear to be denying, then perhaps fades in busy middle life, to return, say, in a sudden premonitory bout of insomnia. One of the supreme secular meditations on death is Larkin's *Aubade*:

> ... *The sure extinction that we travel to*
> *And shall be lost in always. Not to be here,*
> *Not to be anywhere,*
> *And soon; nothing more terrible, nothing more true.*

We confront our mortality in private conversations, in the familiar consolations of religion – 'That vast moth-eaten musical brocade,' thought Larkin, 'Created to pretend we never die.' And we experience it as a creative tension, an enabling paradox in our literature and art: what is depicted, loved, or celebrated cannot last, and the work must try to outlive its creator. Larkin, after all, is now dead. Unless we are a determined, well-organised suicide, we cannot know the date of our demise, but we know the date must fall within a certain window of biological possibility which, as we age, must progressively narrow to its closing point.

Estimating the nature and timing of our *collective* demise, not a lecture-roomful, but the end of civilisation, of the entire human project, is even less certain – it might happen in the next hundred years, or not happen in two thousand, or happen with imperceptible slowness. The fossil records show us that, overwhelmingly, most species are extinct. But in the face of that unknowability, there has often flourished powerful certainty about the approaching end. Throughout recorded history people have mesmerised themselves with stories which predict the date and manner of our whole-scale destruction, often rendered meaningful by ideas of divine punishment and ultimate redemption; the end of life on earth, the end or last days, end time, the apocalypse.

Many of these stories are highly specific accounts of the future and are devoutly believed. Contemporary apocalyptic movements, Christian or Islamic, some violent, some not, all appear to share fantasies of a violent end, and they affect our politics profoundly. The apocalyptic mind can be demonising – that is to say there are other groups, other faiths, that it despises for worshipping false gods, and these believers of course will not be saved from the fires of hell.

And the apocalyptic mind tends to be totalitarian – that these are intact, all-encompassing ideas founded in longing and supernatural belief, immune to evidence or its lack, and well protected against the implications of fresh data. Consequently, moments of unintentional pathos, even comedy, arise – and perhaps something in our nature is revealed – as the future is constantly having to be rewritten, new anti-Christs, new Beasts, new Babylons, new Whores located, and the old appointments with doom and redemption quickly replaced by the next.

Not even a superficial student of the Christian apocalypse could afford to ignore the work of Norman Cohn. His magisterial *The Pursuit of the Millennium* was published sixty years ago and is a study of a variety of end-time movements that swept through northern Europe between the eleventh and sixteenth centuries. These sects, generally inspired by the symbolism in the Book of Revelation, typically led by a charismatic prophet who emerged from among the artisan class or from the dispossessed, were seized by the notion of an impending end, to be followed by the establishing of the Kingdom of God on earth. In preparation for this, it was believed necessary to slaughter Jews, priests and property owners. Fanatical rabbles, tens-of-thousands-strong, oppressed and often starving and homeless, roamed from town to town, full of wild hope and murderous intent. The authorities, church and lay, would put down these bands with great violence. A few years, or a generation later, with a new leader and faintly different emphasis, a new group would rise up. It is worth remembering that the impoverished mobs that trailed behind the knights of the first Crusades started their journeys by killing Jews in the thousands in the Upper Rhine area. These days, when Muslims of radical tendency pronounce against 'Jews and Crusaders', they should remember that both Jewry and Islam were victims of the Crusades.

What strikes the reader of Cohn's book are the common threads that run between medieval and contemporary apocalyptic thought. First, and in general, the resilience of the end-time forecasts – time and again, for 500 years, the date is proclaimed, nothing happens, and no one feels discouraged from setting another date. Second, the Book of Revelation spawned a literary tradition that kept alive in medieval Europe the fantasy, derived from the Judaic tradition, of divine election. Christians, too, could now be the Chosen People, the saved or the Elect, and no amount of official repression could smother the appeal of this notion to the unprivileged as well as the unbalanced. Third, there looms the figure of a mere man, apparently virtuous, risen to eminence, but in reality seductive and Satanic – he is the anti-Christ, and in the five centuries that Cohen surveys, the role is fulfilled by the Pope, just as it frequently is now.

Finally, there is the boundless adaptability, the undying appeal and fascination of the Book of Revelation itself, the central text of apocalyptic belief. When Christopher Columbus arrived in the Americas, making landfall in the Bahaman islands, he believed he had found, and had been fated to find, the Terrestrial Paradise promised in the Book of Revelation. He believed himself to be implicated in God's planning for the millennial kingdom on earth.

The scholar Daniel Wocjik quotes from Columbus's account of his first journey: 'God made me the messenger of the new heaven and the new earth of which he spoke in the Apocalypse of St John ... and he showed me the spot where to find it.'

Five centuries later, the United States, responsible for more than four-fifths of the world's scientific research and still a land of plenty, can show the world an abundance of opinion polls concerning its religious convictions. The litany will be familiar. A strong majority of Americans say they have never doubted the existence of God and are certain they will be called to answer for their sins. Over half are creationists who believe that the cosmos is 6,000 years old, and are certain that Jesus will return to judge the living and the dead within the next fifty years. In one survey, 12 per cent believed that life on earth has evolved through natural selection without the intervention of supernatural agency.

In general, belief in end-time biblical prophecy, in a world purified by catastrophe and then redeemed and made entirely Christian and free of conflict by the return of Jesus in our lifetime, is stronger in the United States than anywhere on the planet, and extends from marginal, ill-educated, economically deprived groups to college-educated people in the millions, through to governing elites, to the very summits of power. The social scientist J. W. Nelson notes that apocalyptic ideas 'are as American as the hot dog'. Wojcik reminds us of the ripple of anxiety that ran round the world in April 1984 when President Reagan acknowledged that he was greatly interested in the biblical prophecy of imminent Armageddon.

To the secular mind, these survey figures have a titillating quality – one might think of them as a form of atheist's pornography. But one should retain a degree of scepticism. They vary enormously – one poll's 90 per cent is another's 53 per cent. From a respondent's point of view, what is to be gained by categorically denying the existence of God to a complete stranger with a clipboard? Those who tell pollsters they believe that the Bible is the literal word of God from which derive all proper moral precepts, are more likely to be thinking in general terms of love, compassion, and forgiveness rather than of the slave-owning, ethnic cleansing, infanticide and genocide urged at various times by the jealous God of the Old Testament.

Furthermore, the mind is capable of artful compartmentalisations; in one moment, a man might confidently believe in predictions of Armageddon in his lifetime, and in the next, he might pick up the phone to enquire about a savings fund for his grandchildren's college education or approve of long-term measures to slow global warming. Or he might even vote Democrat, as do many Hispanic biblical literalists. In Pennsylvania, Kansas and Ohio, the courts have issued ringing rejections of Intelligent Design, and voters have ejected creationists from school boards. In the celebrated Dover case, Judge John Jones the third, a Bush appointee, handed down a judgment that was not only a scathing dismissal of the prospect of supernatural ideas imported into science classes, but was also an elegant, stirring summary of the project of science in general, and of natural selection in particular, and a sturdy endorsement of the rationalist, Enlightenment values that underlie the Constitution.

Still, the Book of Revelation, the final book of the Bible, and perhaps its most bizarre, certainly one of its most lurid, remains important in the United States, just as it once was in medieval Europe. The book is also known as the Apocalypse – and we should be clear about the meaning of this word, which is derived from the Greek word for revelation. Apocalypse, which has become synonymous with 'catastrophe', actually refers to the literary form in which an individual describes what has been revealed to him by a supernatural being. There was a long Jewish tradition of prophecy, and there were hundreds if not thousands of seers like John of Patmos between the second century BC and the first century AD. Many other Christian apocalypses were deprived of canonical authority in the second century AD. Revelation most likely survived because its author was confused with John, the Beloved Disciple. It is interesting to speculate how different medieval European history, and indeed the history of religion in Europe and the United States, would have been if the Book of Revelation had also failed, as it nearly did, to be retained in the Bible we now know.

THE SCHOLARLY CONSENSUS dates Revelation to 95 or 96 AD. Little is known of its author beyond the fact that he is certainly not the apostle John. The occasion of writing appears to be the persecution of Christians under the Roman emperor Domitian. This was only a generation before the Romans sacked the Second Temple in Jerusalem and is therefore identified with the Babylonians who had destroyed the First Temple centuries earlier. The general purpose quite likely was to give hope and consolation to the faithful in the certainty that their tribulations would end, that the Kingdom of God would prevail. Ever since the influential twelfth-century historian, Joachim of Fiore, Revelation has been seen, within various traditions of gathering complexity and divergence, as an overview of human history whose last stage we are now in; alternatively, and this is especially relevant to the postwar United States, as an account purely of those last days. For centuries, within the Protestant tradition, the anti-Christ was identified with the Pope, or with the Catholic Church in general. In recent decades, the honour has been bestowed on the Soviet Union, the European Union, or secularism and atheists. For many millennial dispensationalists, international peacemakers, who risk delaying the final struggle by sowing concord among nations – the United Nations, along with the World Council of Churches, have been seen as Satanic forces.

THE CAST OR contents of Revelation in its contemporary representations has all the colourful gaudiness of a children's computer fantasy game – earthquakes and fires, thundering horses and their riders, angels blasting away on trumpets, magic vials, Jezebel, a red dragon and other mythical beasts, and a scarlet woman. Another familiar aspect is the potency of numbers – seven each of seals, heads of beasts, candlesticks, stars, lamps, trumpets, angels, and vials; then four riders, four beasts with seven heads, ten horns, ten crowns, four-and-twenty elders, twelve tribes with twelve thousand members . . . and finally, most resonantly, spawning nineteen centuries of dark tomfoolery, 'Here is wisdom. Let him that hath understanding count the number of the beast; for it is the number of a man; and his number is six hundred, three score and six.' To many minds, 666 bristles with significance. The Internet is stuffed with tremulous speculation about supermarket barcodes, implanted chips, numerical codes for the names of world leaders. However, the oldest known record of this famous verse, from the Oxyrhynchus site, gives the number as 616, as does the Zurich Bible. I have the impression that any number would do. One senses in the arithmetic of prophecy the yearnings of a systematising mind, bereft of the experimental scientific underpinnings that were to give such human tendencies their rich expression many centuries later. Astrology gives a similar impression of numerical obsession operating within a senseless void.

But Revelation has endured in an age of technology and scepticism. Not many works of literature, not even the *Odyssey* of Homer, can boast such wide appeal over such an expanse of time. One celebrated case of this rugged durability is that of William Miller, the nineteenth-century farmer who became a prophet and made a set of intricate calculations, based on a line in verse 14 of the Book of Daniel: 'unto two thousand and three hundred days; then shall the sanctuary be cleansed.' Counting for various reasons this utterance to date from 457 BC, and understanding one prophetic day to be the equivalent of a year, Miller came to the conclusion that the last of days would occur in 1843. Some of Miller's followers refined the calculations further to 22 October.

After nothing happened on that day, the year was quickly revised to 1844, to take into account the year zero. The faithful Millerites gathered in their thousands to wait. One may not share the beliefs, but still understand the mortifying disenchantment. One eyewitness wrote,

> [We] confidently expected to see Jesus Christ and all the holy angels with him . . . and that our trials and sufferings with our earthly pilgrimage would close and we should be caught up to meet our coming Lord . . . and thus we looked for our coming Lord until the bell tolled twelve at midnight. The day had then passed and our disappointment became a certainty. Our fondest hopes and expectations were blasted, and such a spirit of weeping came over us as I never experienced before. It seemed that the loss of all our earthly friends could have been no comparison. We wept, and wept, till the day dawn.

One means of dealing with the disillusionment was to give it a title – the Great Disappointment – duly capitalised. More importantly, according to Kenneth Newport's account of the Waco siege, the very next day after the Disappointment, one Millerite leader in Port Gibson, New York, by the name of Hiram Edson had a vision as he walked along, a sudden revelation that 'the cleansing of the sanctuary' referred to events not on earth, but in heaven. Jesus had taken his place in the heavenly holy of holies. The date had been right all along: it was simply the *place* they had got wrong. This 'masterstroke', as Newport calls it, this 'theological lifeline', removed the whole affair into a realm immune to disproof. The Great Disappointment was explained, and many Millerites were drawn, with hope still strong in their hearts, into the beginnings of the Seventh Day Adventist movement – which was to become one of the most successful churches in the United States.

Note the connections between this tendency and the medieval sects that Cohn describes – the strong emphasis on the Book of Revelation, the looming proximity of the end, the strict division between the faithful remnant who keep the Sabbath and those who join the ranks of the 'fallen', of the anti-Christ, identified with the Pope whose title, Vicarius Filii Dei (vicar of the son of God), apparently has a numerical value of 666.

I mention Hiram Edson's morning-after masterstroke to illustrate the resilience of end-time thought. For centuries, it has regarded the end as 'soon' – if not next week, then within a year or two. The end has not come, and yet no one is discomfited for long. New prophets, and soon, a new generation, set about the calculations, and always manage to find the end looming within their own lifetime. The million-sellers like Hal Lindsey predicted the end of the world all through the seventies, eighties and nineties – and today, business has never been better. There is a hunger for this news, and perhaps we glimpse here something in our nature, something of our deeply held notions of time, and our own insignificance against the intimidating vastness of eternity or the age of the universe – on the human scale there is little difference. We have need of a plot, a narrative to shore up our irrelevance in the flow of things.

In *The Sense of an Ending*, Frank Kermode suggests that the enduring quality, the vitality of the Book of Revelation suggests a 'consonance with our more naïve requirements of fiction'. We are born, as we will die, in the middle of things, in the 'middest'. To make sense of our span, we need what he calls 'fictive concords with origins and ends. "The End", in the grand sense, as we imagine it, will reflect our irreducibly intermediary expectations.' What could grant us more meaning against the abyss of time than to identify our own personal demise with the purifying annihilation of all that is? Kermode quotes Wallace Stevens: 'it is one of the peculiarities of the imagination that it is always at the end of an era'. Even our notions of decadence contain the hopes of renewal; the religious-minded, as well as the most secular, looked on the transition to the year 2000 as inescapably significant, even if all the atheists did was to party a little harder. It was inevitably a transition, the passing of an old age into the new – and who is to say now that Osama bin Laden did not disappoint, whether we mourned at the dawn of the new millennium with the bereaved among the ruins of lower Manhattan, or danced for joy, as some did, in East Jerusalem?

Islamic eschatology from its very beginnings embraced the necessity of violently conquering the world and gathering up souls to the faith before the expected hour of judgment – a notion that has risen and fallen over the centuries, but in past decades has received new impetus from Islamist revivalist movements. It is partly a mirror image of the Protestant Christian tradition (a world made entirely Islamic, with Jesus as Muhammad's lieutenant), partly a fantasy of the inevitable return of 'sacred space', the Caliphate, that includes most of Spain, parts of France, the entire Middle East, right up to the borders of China. As with the Christian scheme, Islam foretells of the destruction or conversion of the Jews.

PROPHECY BELIEF IN Judaism, the original source for both the Islamic and Christian eschatologies, is surprisingly weaker – perhaps a certain irony in the relationship between Jews and their god is unfriendly to end-time belief, but it lives on vigorously enough in the Lubavitch movement and various Israeli settler groups, and of course is centrally concerned with divine entitlement to disputed lands.

WE SHOULD ADD to the mix more recent secular apocalyptic beliefs – the certainty that the world is inevitably doomed through nuclear exchange, viral epidemics, meteorites, population growth or environmental degradation. Where these calamities are posed as mere possibilities in an open-ended future that might be headed off by wise human agency, we cannot consider them as apocalyptic. They are minatory, they are calls to action. But when they are presented as unavoidable outcomes driven by ineluctable forces of history or innate human failings, they share much with their religious counterparts – though they lack the demonising, cleansing, redemptive aspects, and are without the kind of supervision of a supernatural entity that might give benign meaning and purpose to a mass extinction. Clearly, fatalism is common to both camps, and both, reasonably enough, are much concerned with a nuclear holocaust, which to the prophetic believers illuminates in retrospect biblical passages that once seemed obscure. Hal Lindsey, pre-eminent among the popularisers of American apocalyptic thought, writes,

Zechariah 14:12 predicts that 'their flesh will be consumed from their bones, their eyes burned out of their sockets, and their tongues consumed out of their mouths while they stand on their feet'. For hundreds of years students of Bible prophecy have wondered what kind of plague could produce such instant ravaging of humans while still on their feet. Until the event of the atomic bomb such a thing was not humanly possible. But now everything Zecheriah predicted could come true in a thermonuclear exchange!

Two other movements, now mercifully defeated or collapsed, provide a further connection between religious and secular apocalypse – so concluded Norman Cohn in the closing pages of *The Pursuit of the Millennium*. The genocidal tendency among the apocalyptic medieval movements faded somewhat after 1500. Vigorous end-time belief continued, of course, in the Puritan and Calvinist movements, the Millerites, as we have seen, and in the American Great Awakening, Mormonism, Jehovah's Witnesses and the Adventist movement.

The murderous tradition, however, did not die away completely. It survived the passing of centuries in various sects, various outrages, to emerge in the European twentieth century transformed, revitalised, secularised, but still recognisable in what Cohn depicts as the essence of apocalyptic thinking:

> the tense expectation of a final, decisive struggle in which a world tyranny will be overthrown by a "chosen people" and through which the world will be renewed and history brought to its consummation. The will of god was transformed in the twentieth century into the will of history, but the essential demand remained, as it still does today – to purify the world by destroying the agents of corruption.

The dark reveries of Nazism about the Jews shared much with the murderous anti-Semitic demonology of medieval times. An important additional element, imported from Russia, was *The Protocols of the Elders of Zion*, the 1905 Tsarist police forgery, elevated by Hitler and others into a racist ideology. (It's interesting to note how the *Protocols* has re-emerged as a central text for Islamists, frequently quoted on websites, and sold in street book stalls across the Middle East.) The Third Reich and its dream of a thousand-year rule was derived, in a form of secular millennial usurpation, directly from Revelation. Cohn draws our attention to the apocalyptic language of *Mein Kampf*:

> If our people . . . fall victims to these Jewish tyrants of the nations with their lust for blood and gold, the

whole earth will sink down ... if Germany frees itself from this embrace, this greatest of dangers for the peoples can be regarded as vanquished for all the earth.

In Marxism in its Soviet form, Cohn also found a continuation of the old millenarian tradition of prophecy, of the final violent struggle to eliminate the agents of corruption – this time it is the bourgeoisie who will be vanquished by the proletariat in order to enable the withering away of the state and usher in the peaceable kingdom. 'The kulak ... is prepared to strangle and massacre hundreds of thousands of workers ... Ruthless war must be waged on the kulaks! Death to them!' Thus spoke Lenin, and his word, like Hitler's, became deed.

Thirty years ago, we might have been able to convince ourselves that contemporary religious apocalyptic thought was a harmless remnant of a more credulous, superstitious, pre-scientific age, now safely behind us. But today prophecy belief, particularly within the Christian and Islamic traditions, is a force in our contemporary history, a medieval engine driving our modern moral, geo-political and military concerns. Various gods – and they are certainly not one and the same god – who in the past directly addressed Abraham, Paul, or Muhammad, among others, now indirectly address us through the internet and television news. These different gods have wound themselves inextricably around our political differences.

Our secular and scientific culture has not replaced or barely challenged these mutually incompatible, supernatural thought systems. Scientific method, scepticism, or rationality in general, has yet to find an overarching narrative of sufficient power, simplicity and wide appeal to compete with the old stories that give meaning to people's lives. Natural selection is a powerful, elegant and economic explicator of life on earth in all its diversity, and perhaps it contains the seeds of a rival creation myth that would have the added power of being true – but it awaits its inspired synthesiser, its poet, its Milton. E. O. Wilson has suggested an ethics divorced from religion, and derived instead from what he calls biophilia, our innate and profound connection to our natural environment – but one man alone cannot make a moral system. Climate science may speak of rising sea levels and global temperatures, with figures that it refines in line with new data, but on the human future it cannot compete with the luridness and, above all, with the meaningfulness of the prophecies in the Book of Daniel, or Revelation. Reason and myth remain uneasy bedfellows.

Rather than presenting a challenge, science has in

obvious ways strengthened apocalyptic thinking. It has provided us with the means to destroy ourselves and our civilisation completely in less than a couple of hours, or to spread a fatal virus around the globe in a couple of days. And our spiraling technologies of destruction and their ever-greater availability have raised the possibility that true believers, with all their unworldly passion, their prayerful longing for the end-times to begin, could help nudge the ancient prophecies towards fulfillment. Daniel Wojcik, in his study of apocalyptic thought in America, quotes a letter by the singer Pat Boone addressed to fellow Christians. All-out nuclear war is what he appears to have had in mind.

> My guess is that there isn't a thoughtful Christian alive who doesn't believe we are living at the end of history. I don't know how that makes you feel, but it gets me pretty excited. Just think about actually seeing, as the apostle Paul wrote it, the Lord Himself descending from heaven with a shout! Wow! And the signs that it's about to happen are everywhere.

If the possibility of a willed nuclear catastrophe appears too pessimistic or extravagant, or hilarious, consider the case of another individual, remote from Pat Boone – former President Ahmadinejad of Iran. His much reported remark about wiping Israel off the face of the earth may have been mere bluster of the kind you could hear any Friday or Sunday in a thousand mosques and churches around the world. But this posturing, coupled with his nuclear ambitions, become more worrying when set in the context of his end-time beliefs. In Jamkaran, a village not far from the holy city of Qom, a small mosque underwent a 20-million-dollar expansion that was driven forward by Ahmadinejad's office during his incumbency. Within the Shi'ite apocalyptic tradition, the Twelfth Imam, the Mahdi, who disappeared in the ninth century, is expected to reappear in a well behind the mosque. His re-emergence will signify the beginning of the end days. He will lead the battle against the Dajjal, the Islamic version of the antiChrist, and, with Jesus as his follower, will establish the global Dar el Salam, the dominion of peace, under Islam. Ahmadinejad extended the mosque to receive the Mahdi. Pilgrims by the thousands immediately visited the shrine, for the President reportedly told his cabinet that he expected the visitation within two years.

Or again, consider the celebrated case of the red heifer, or calf. On the Temple Mount in Jerusalem, the end-time stories of Judaism, Christianity, and Islam converge in both interlocking and mutually exclusive ways that are potentially explosive – they form incidentally the material for the American novelist Robert

Stone's fine novel, *Damascus Gate*. What is bitterly contested is not only the past and present, but the future. It is hardly possible to do justice in summary to the complex eschatologies that jostle on this thirty-five-acre patch of land. The stories themselves are familiar. For the Jews, the Mount – the biblical Mount Moriah – is the site of the First Temple, destroyed by Nebuchadnezzar in 586 BC, and of the Second Temple destroyed by the Romans in 70 AD. According to tradition, and of particular interest to various controversial groups, including the Temple Institute, the Messiah, when he comes at last, will occupy the Third Temple. But that cannot be built, and therefore the Messiah will not come, without the sacrifice of a perfectly unblemished red calf.

For Muslims, the Mount is the site of the Dome of the Rock, built over the location of the two temples and enclosing the very spot from which Muhammad departed on his Night Journey to heaven – leaving as he stepped upwards a revered footprint in the rock. In the prophetic tradition, the Dajjal will be a Jew who leads a devastating war against Islam. Attempts to bless a foundation stone of a new temple are seen as highly provocative, for this implies the destruction of the mosque. The symbolism surrounding Ariel Sharon's visit to the Mount in September 2000 remains a matter of profoundly different interpretation by Muslims and Jews. And if lives were not at stake, the Christian fundamentalist contribution to this volatile mix would seem amusingly cynical. These prophetic believers are certain that Jesus will return at the height of the battle of Armageddon, but his thousand-year reign, which will ensure the conversion of Jews and Muslims to Christianity, or their extinction, cannot begin until the Third Temple is built.

And so it came about that a cattle-breeding operation emerged in Israel with the help of Texan Christian fundamentalist ranchers to promote the birth of the perfect, unspotted red calf, and thereby, we have to assume, bring the end days a little closer. In 1997 there was great excitement, as well as press mockery, when one promising candidate appeared. Months later, this cherished young cow nicked its rump on a barbed wire fence, causing white hairs to grow at the site of the wound and earning instant disqualification. Another red calf appeared in 2002 to general acclaim, and then again, later disappointment. In the tight squeeze of history, religion and politics that surrounds the Temple Mount, the calf is a minor item. But the search for it, and the hope and longing that surround it, illustrate the dangerous tendency among prophetic believers to bring on the cataclysm that they think will lead to a form of paradise on earth. The reluctance of the current US administration to pursue an even-handed policy towards a peace settlement in the Israel-Palestine dispute may owe as much to the pressures of nationalist Jewish groups as to the eschatology of Christian fundamentalists.

Periods of uncertainty in human history, of rapid, bewildering change and of social unrest appear to give these old stories greater weight. It does not need a novelist to tell you that where a narrative has a beginning, it needs an end. Where there is a creation myth, there must be a final chapter. Where a god makes the world, it remains in his power to unmake it. When human weakness or wickedness is apparent, there will be guilty fantasies of supernatural retribution. When people are profoundly frustrated, either materially or spiritually, there will be dreams of the perfect society where all conflicts are resolved and all needs are met.

That much we can understand or politely pretend to understand. But the problem of fatalism remains. In a nuclear age, and in an age of serious environmental degradation, apocalyptic belief creates a serious second-order danger. The precarious logic of self-interest that saw us through the Cold War would collapse if the leaders of one nuclear state came to welcome, or ceased to fear, mass death. These words of Ayatollah Khomeini are quoted approvingly in an Iranian eleventh grade textbook: 'Either we shake one another's hands in joy at the victory of Islam in the world, or all of us will turn to eternal life and martyrdom. In both cases, victory and success are ours.' If I were a believer, I think I would prefer to be in Jesus's camp. He is reported by Matthew to have said, 'No one knows about that day or hour, not even the angels in heaven, nor the Son, but only the Father.'

Even a sceptic can find in the historical accumulation of religious expression joy, fear, love and above all, seriousness. I return to Philip Larkin – an atheist who also knew the moment and the nature of transcendence. In 'Church Going' he writes:

A serious house on serious earth it is,
In whose blent air all our compulsions meet,
Are recognised, and robed as destinies.

And how could one be more serious than the writer of this prayer for the interment of the dead, from *The Book of Common Prayer*, an incantation of bleak, existential beauty, even more so in its beautiful setting by Henry Purcell: 'Man that is born of a woman hath but a short time to live, and is full of misery. He cometh up, and is cut down, like a flower; he fleeth as it were a shadow, and never continueth in one stay.'

Ultimately, apocalyptic belief is a function of faith – that luminous inner conviction that needs no recourse to evidence. It is customary to pose against immoveable faith the engines of reason, but in this instance I would prefer that delightful human impulse – curiosity, the hallmark of mental freedom. Organised religion has always had – and I put this mildly – a troubled relationship with curiosity. Islam's distrust, at least in the past 200 years, is best expressed by its attitude to those whose faith falls away, to apostates who are drawn to other religions or to none at all. In recent times, in 1975, the mufti of Saudi Arabia, Bin Baz, in a fatwa, quoted by Shmuel Bar, ruled as followed: 'Those who claim that the earth is round and moving around the Sun are apostates and their blood can be shed and their property can be taken in the name of God.' Bin Baz rescinded this judgment ten years later. Mainstream Islam routinely prescribes punishment for apostates that ranges from ostracism to beatings to death. To enter one of the many websites where Muslim apostates anonymously exchange views is to encounter a world of brave and terrified men and women who have succumbed to their disaffection and intellectual curiosity.

And Christians should not feel smug. The first commandment – on pain of death if we were to take the matter literally – is 'Thou shalt have no other gods before me.' In the fourth century, St Augustine put the matter well for Christianity, and his view prevailed for a long time: 'There is another form of temptation, even more fraught with danger. This is the disease of curiosity. It is this which drives us to try and discover the secrets of nature which are beyond our understanding, which can avail us nothing, and which man should not wish to learn.'

And yet it is curiosity, scientific curiosity, that has delivered us genuine, testable knowledge of the world and contributed to our understanding of our place within it and of our nature and condition. This knowledge has a beauty of its own, and it can be terrifying. We are barely beginning to grasp the implications of what we have relatively recently learned. And what exactly have we learned? I draw here from and adapt a Stephen Pinker essay on his ideal of a university: among other things we have learned that our planet is a minute speck in an inconceivably vast cosmos; that our species has existed for a tiny fraction of the history of the earth; that humans are primates; that the mind is the activity of an organ that runs by physiological processes; that there are methods for ascertaining the truth that can force us to conclusions which violate common sense, sometimes radically, so at scales very large and very small; that precious and widely held beliefs, when subjected to empirical tests, are often cruelly falsified; that we cannot create energy or use it without loss.

As things stand, after more than a century of research in a number of fields, we have no evidence at all that the future can be predicted. Better to look directly to the past, to its junkyard of unrealised futures, for it is curiosity about history that should give end-time believers reasonable pause when they reflect that they stand on a continuum, a long and unvarying thousand-year tradition that has fantasised imminent salvation for themselves and perdition for the rest. On one of the countless end-time/rapture sites that litter the Web, there is a section devoted to Frequently Asked Questions. One is: When the Lord comes, what will happen to the children of other faiths? The answer is staunch: 'Ungodly parents only bring judgment to their children.' In the light of this, one might conclude that end-time faith is probably immune to the lessons of history.

If we do destroy ourselves, we can be sure that the general reaction will be terror, and grief at the pointlessness of it all, rather than rapture. Within living memory we have come very close to extinguishing our civilisation when, in October 1962, Soviet ships carrying nuclear warheads to installations in Cuba confronted a blockade by the US Navy, and the world waited to discover whether Nikita Khrushchev would order his convoy home. It is remarkable how little of that terrifying event survives in public memory, in modern folklore. In the vast literature the Cuban Missile Crisis has spawned – military, political, diplomatic – there is very little on its effect at the time on ordinary lives, in homes, schools and the workplace, on the fear and widespread numb incomprehension in the population at large. That fear has not passed into the national narrative, here or anywhere else, as vividly as one might expect. As Spencer Weart put it, 'When the crisis ended, most people turned their attention away as swiftly as a child who lifts up a rock, sees something slimy underneath, and drops the rock back.' Perhaps the assassination of President Kennedy the following year helped obscure the folk memory of the Missile Crisis. His murder in Dallas became a marker in the history of instantaneous globalized news transmission – a huge proportion of the world's population seemed to be able to recall where they were when they heard the news. Conflating these two events, Christopher Hitchens opened an essay on the Cuban Missile Crisis with the words – 'Like everyone else of my generation, I can remember exactly where I was standing and what I was doing on the day that President John Fitzgerald Kennedy nearly killed me.' Heaven did not beckon during those tense hours of the crisis. Instead, as Hitchens observes, 'It brought the world to the best view it has had yet of the gates of hell.'

I began with the idea of photography as the inventory of mortality, and I will end with a photograph of a group death. It shows fierce flames and smoke rising from a building in Waco, Texas, at the end of a fifty-one-day siege in 1993. The group inside was the Branch Davidians, an offshoot of the Seventh Day Adventists. Its leader, David Koresh, was a man steeped in biblical, end-time theology, convinced that America was Babylon, the agent of Satan, arriving in the form of the Bureau of Alcohol, Tobacco, and Firearms and the FBI to destroy the Sabbath-keeping remnant who would emerge from the cleansing, suicidal fire to witness the dawn of a new Kingdom. Here is Susan Sontag's 'posthumous irony' indeed, as medieval Europe recreated itself in the form of a charismatic man, a messiah, a messenger of God, the bearer of the perfect truth, who exercised sexual power over his female followers and persuaded them to bear his children in order to begin a 'Davidian' line. In that grim inferno, children, their mothers and other followers died. Even more died two years later when Timothy McVeigh, exacting revenge against the government for its attack on Waco, committed his slaughter in Oklahoma City. It is not for nothing that one of the symptoms in a developing psychosis, noted and described by psychiatrists, is 'religiosity'.

Have we really reached a stage in public affairs when it is no longer too obvious to say that all the evidence of the past and all the promptings of our precious rationality suggest that our future is not fixed? We have no reason to believe that there are dates inscribed in heaven or hell. We may yet destroy ourselves; we might scrape through. Confronting that uncertainty is the obligation of our maturity and our only spur to wise action. The believers should know in their hearts by now that, even if they are right and there actually is a benign and watchful personal God, he is, as all the daily tragedies, all the dying children attest, a reluctant intervener. The rest of us, in the absence of any evidence to the contrary, know that it is highly improbable that there is anyone up there at all. Either way, in this case it hardly matters who is wrong – there will be no one to save us but ourselves.

Payne Lecture, Stanford University, 2007

5

The Self

Is there a mental entity quite so paradoxical as the self? Overwhelmingly self-evident, and yet teasingly elusive. On waking of a morning we step into it, or it into us, as though into a pair of comfortable old shoes. Or, more accurately, we wake and the shoes are already on our feet. Others wake into very uncomfortable shoes. An unfortunate, pathological few, wake barefoot to find themselves in a horribly familiar torture chamber. Even in sleep we don't quite escape the self, for in our dreams, it's the witness or participant, often both at once. And yet we have problems defining this self. Certainly, philosophers do. And the task of describing it, conveying it to other selves — selves we cannot by definition ever enter — is intricate, never complete and only began in our literature, so I'll want to argue later on, in a methodical, extended or self-conscious way, in early modernity — by which I mean, broadly, the sixteenth century. And by 'our' I take a general Eurocentric view with its roots in the Graeco-Roman world.

We might want to conflate the self with consciousness itself, but we know that's not an exact fit: not all parts of the self are available to us all the time. Consciousness surely entails *awareness* of the self, and selfhood is the recipient of all that consciousness offers, but it's not the self — or, it's not the whole self, it's not the self *itself* And nor, quite, is character, which has a third person quality, useful for describing others, or for understanding and predicting their behaviour, but lacking the felt, subjective quality of selfhood. There's no shortage of loose synonyms — the heart, the soul, the mind, individuality. One approximation might be the particular meaning of the word 'life' — as in 'inner life'. It's your life you resume on waking — and not only its outward manifestation in work or relationships; it's what you have to live inside. The self as experienced life is what James Fenton summons in a celebrated poem. Its disconsolate narrator declares in the opening line, 'I took my life and threw it on the skip,' Later, the narrator finds someone else's life lying sodden on that same skip, takes it home, dries it by the stove. 'I tried it on. It fitted like a glove.' It's an old self the unhappy narrator has abandoned, it's a new self he happily assumes. The least contented of us might protest — if only the self could be so easily discarded.

But a life in Fenton's sense is still not quite a self. We can change our lives, and our selves mutate over time, but there's something enduring or inescapable about the self. Recreational drugs, including alcohol, might lift you clear for a little while, but your old self, the one you had before you went out to the skip, will be waiting for you when you get back. And though we live daily within the bounds of selfhood, self-evidently, it steps outside its own limits to wonder about itself. Think of the language available to us that turns recursively on the self — self-loving, self-doubting, self-important, self-denying , self-possessed — the list is long and only selves could have compiled it. When Bob Dylan sings to a departing lover, 'Yer gonna make me give myself a good talking to,' we know what he means. We also know that the one who'll be doing the talking will also be obliged to do the listening.

A neuroscientist will tell you — with the *self-assurance* that was once the prerogative of a priest — that you won't find the self lodged in any particular locus in the brain, like the pineal gland was in Descarte's description of the soul. There is no crouching, watchful homunculus. Instead, the self is everywhere and nowhere in the brain, spread across vastly complex neural networks. But it's well-established that traumas to the pre-frontal cortex may cause radical alterations in the subjective sense of self. Lesions that compromise or nearly obliterate autobiographical memory will massively disrupt the constructs of selfhood, suggesting that time and memory and continuity are essential ingredients of what it means to be a self.

Here we enter another contested region. The self as a form of narrative, an unfolding story we tell ourselves, has come to constitute the contemporary orthodoxy. No one has written better on this, or gathered together the so-called 'narrativist' sources so thoroughly as the philosopher, Galen Strawson, even as he remains deeply sceptical of the claims or, at least, of the assumption that they apply to everyone. By his account, there's no shortage of forceful, articulate proponents both within the humanities and in pscychotherapy, of the view that we are the book that we write ourselves. Here are just a few of Strawson's 'narrativists': 'Each of us constructs and lives a "narrative" ... this narrative is us...' says Oliver Sachs; 'Self is a perpetually rewritten story,' writes Jerome Bruner in The Remembered Self; and from various other scholarly sources — a person 'creates his identity by forming an autobiographical narrative' ; we are all 'virtuoso novelists' ; 'the chief fictional character at the centre of that autobiography is the self.' .

One of the attractions of this view is that it bestows a flattering degree of agency. We're empowered by a sense that we are our own deliberate constructions. The American novelist Mary McCarthy wrote, '... you finally begin in some sense to make and choose the self you want.' Germaine Greer goes even further: 'human beings have an inalienable right to invent themselves.'

Naturally, the innate, universal construct of authored selfhood appeals to novelists. You'll hear us on panels at literary festivals, routinely asserting that we are, all of us, above all else, story-telling creatures, that we write ourselves into existence, and that without these self-stories we experience a form of mental death and the necessary dissolution of our humanity. But it's worth remembering that novelists are paid to make things up. Furthermore, you'll hear from many walks of life — from geneticists, architects, physicists, town-planners — that *their* particular career choices encompass the basics, the essentials of what it means to be human. We all like to think we're not only important, but *necessary* Novelists are, naturally defensive on that count.

Personally, I was for a good while a guiltily tepid narrativist on those panels. I felt I ought to be more of a comrade and join in enthusiastically. My unease derived from two sources — a lack of belief in the free will necessary to allow me to write or construct a self. I didn't choose my childhood, I didn't choose my genes, I didn't choose the self I've ended up with. At the same time, I was happy to accept free will as a necessary illusion: we 'own' a consciousness and we therefore must take responsibility for it. Secondly, at any given time, I don't remember all that much. Childhood, adolescence, early adulthood — mere scraps, not in reliable sequence, available only with effort, or in response to focussed questions, and certainly not part of some daily experienced 'story'. I've always felt humbled confronting the novels of Saul Bellow or John Updike. Dickens is another great example. Their novels teem with materials, minor and major characters, smells, voices, locations drawn from their early lives — a vast compendium of rich experience they could effortlessly summon and fictionalise.

Unlike Updike, I don't remember all the girls' playground skipping rhymes, or the sweetshop lady's name, or the smell of the breath of the first dentist to examine my teeth. Given these deficiencies, it was a relief, even a liberation ,to read Strawson, and to read him quoting Bill Blattner: 'We are not texts. Our histories are not narratives. Life is not literature.' As Strawson writes, 'Somebody had to say it. ' He for one doesn't experience his self as a self-manufactured story, but as episodic, somewhat chaotic, bounded by discrete moments, in a procession of successive presents. He claims a 'perfectly respectable degree of knowledge about his past but doesn't think an autobiographical narrative plays 'any significant role in how I experience the world.' He invokes Henry James's 'great shambles of life'. Strawson doesn't dispute the narrativist's version of their inner life, (though he wonders if its proponents are reporting their experience accurately). He simply wants to say that he and others are not like that.

He prefers to divide us, in time-honoured fashion, into two sorts — 'those who have the emotion of authorship with respect to their thoughts, and those who, like myself, have no such emotion and feel that their thoughts are things that just happen.' For the non-narrativist camp, he proves himself again a good archivist of the apt quotation. Here's Emerson: 'We are carried by destiny along life's course looking as grave and knowing [and] as little as the infant who is carried in his wicker coach thro' the street.' Despite his long memory, John Updike writes that he has 'the persistent sensation in my life... that I am just beginning.' Strawson summons Updike again from another essay in which he lamented the insufficiency of biography as a literary form. It 'cannot covey the unearthly innocence that attends, in the perpetual present tense of living, the self that seems the real one.' Strawson can't resist (who can) the often-quoted passage from Virginia Woolf's essay, 'Modern Fiction' . 'Life is not a series of gig lamps symmetrically arranged; life is a luminous halo, a semi-transparent envelope surrounding us from the beginning of consciousness to the end...'

What's missing from many accounts of what constitutes a self is the fact of its embodiment. We are not brains in petri dishes. The experience of being a self is also the experience of having a body in all its familiarity, its growth, decline, gripes and pleasures. That ache in the jaw when you eat ice cream, the mole on your knees that's accompanied you since childhood, the toe that troubles you whenever you walk more than a few miles, the shiver down your spine when you hear a particular piece of music. Or more fundamentally, the sensation of simply being in a body — it's current orientation, the disposition of your limbs.

Updike is good on this, as he is on all the minutiae, the small print of existence. He writes in his essay, On Being a Self Forever, 'When I look up at a blank blue sky, or rest my gaze on a bright surface of snow, I become aware of a fixed pattern of optical imperfections — specks in my vitreous humour like frozen microbes — that float, usually unnoticed, in the field of my seeing.' Then, habitually and extra-corporeally, he has scraps of old songs, bits of off-beat rhymes in his thoughts: 'I'm biding my time' Cause that 's the kinda guy I'm.' When he signs his name his hand tends to freeze at the top of the 'd' . There's a spot on his palm, caused long before, when he was at high school and accidentally stabbed himself with a pencil. When he raises the first knuckle of the index finger of his left hand, he notices a faint bad smell, however much he washes his hands. It's somehow satisfying. Waking thoughts tend to be absurd: do his fingernails need cutting? Why does his shoe lace keep coming undone? Rehashed anxieties, blurred recollections — all these data comprise his intimate self, the bedrock below his 'more or less acceptable social, sexual and professional performance.'

These are the intimate details peculiar to one man's sense

of an embodied self. Updike is contemplating eternity in this essay and what it would mean to have this self and all its peculiarities 'persist forever, to outlast the atomic universe.' There is, he (a believer) concedes, some absurdity in this for us who live our lives in a condition of constant change. And the mention of change brings me to confront two opposing elements of selfhood — continuity and transience. It was John Locke who famously connected identity, a sense of selfhood, with continuity through time. 'to find wherein personal identity consists, we must consider what person stands for; — which, I think, is a thinking intelligent being, that has reason and reflection, and can consider itself as itself, the same thinking thing, in different times and places... it is the same self now it was then; and it is by the same self with this present one that now reflects on it...'

Here's the common paradox of the self — we acknowledge that we change through time, that our five year old self, our fourteen year self were profoundly different from our present self, and yet that five and fourteen year old year old have a claim on us we can't shake off. In Updike's sense of it, 'we age and leave behind this litter of dead irrecoverable selves.' I would disagree — never quite dead, however irrecoverable, never left behind, even if forgotten. A frail thread of causation, consequence and randomness ties us to our earlier selves. Every day, every hour and second of it, every heart beat, lead like stepping stones from the toddler to the old woman. A man still stands trial for the murder he committed thirty years ago. We own that old self and remain responsible for all its acts. Otherwise, the criminal justice system would collapse. So it is that an author at public events must answer questions about a story or a novel he wrote fifty years ago. The obligation is there clearly, for he doesn't object when the occasional royalty payment for that book arrives. But that won't rescue him from feeling a fraud, an imposter. That book is not the product of his current self. Its alien sentences or surprising subject matter could so easily have been created by someone else. Hence Philip Larkin's dislike of public appearances, which he described in terms of going around 'pretending to be myself.'

Finally, in this brief survey of the elements of selfhood, we confront the one that's most obvious — the inhering, constant, present tense thinker or receiver of thoughts, to whom pains and pleasures, dreams and desires occur; in Locke's words 'that conscious thinking thing... capable of happiness or misery, and so is concerned for itself, as far as that consciousness extends.' The screen onto which sense data fall, core of identity, the one for whom we blush, of whom we are proud or ashamed, or, from Woolf's same essay, recipient of 'myriad impressions — trivial, fantastic, evanescent, or engraved with the sharpness of steel. From all sides they come, an incessant shower of innumerable atoms; as they fall... they shape themselves into the life of Monday or

Tuesday...'

How might we pull these elements of a self together? Think of a Monday morning walk from your home to the work. The feel of the pavement under your feet, the familiarity of your own stride, the pleasant contact with fresh October air. Familiar sounds and sights of rush hour. Scraps of thought that lie beyond your habitual registering of traffic and passers-by. These scattered thoughts seem to occur unprompted, and yet, seem somehow under your control. The thought of an unfulfilled task, vague anticipation of a friend's visit, some sexual memory or desire or ambition goes by like the floater in Updike's vitreous humor; a quick recall of last night's wakefulness, your tongue warily probes a tooth and you think about the dentist. Suffused through all of this, the ghostly fact, held just below the level of thought, are your immediate intentions — getting to work on time, of what must be done when you get there. An unruly voice, another self, tells you, as it has many times before, that it's time you chucked the whole lot in. Cut loose while you're still young! But you can't, says the self that's taking you to work. You have obligations.

Perhaps you meet an old friend and you stop to talk. Automatically, you're attempting to read her mind by way of her facial expression, gestures, posture and content of what she's saying and the tone in which she says it. Crucially, as you converse, you're seeing yourself reflected back to you. Reciprocally, she's doing the same. That self you think of as being so private also takes its form, its shadings of self-worth, from others.

* * *

The anatomically modern human brain in all its cognitive glory has stalked the planet for 200 thousand years, perhaps far less. From skull fractures and other bone traumas we know that early humans lived violent lives. Life expectancy was less than 25 years. But we can know little of the private experiences of the accumulated dead that lie behind us except for what certain individuals cared to write down. For that, we would have to wait for means of cultural transmission, the invention of writing, a mere five and a half thousand years ago.

Rendering private experience was not a pressing concern of the earliest writers. The deciphering of our most ancient texts — Sumerian, Babylonian, ancient Egyptian, reveals civil laws, praise of gods or kings or heroes, religious observances, mercantile reckonings, astronomical observations, floods, droughts, harvests and wars. Cuneiform does not afford us even a glimpse of a rendering of subjectivity. We know next to nothing about the inner life of ancient Egyptians

Coming forward in time into classical antiquity, we see a mental landscape in which the representation of the private self might be described as points of widely spaced light, like the modern countryside seen from a mountaintop —

separated, disconnected points of light representing moments of subjective portrayal, of intimate human truth. They stand out against a background of warrior heroes and their deeds, their villainous opponents, moral exemplars, of men and women battling against their fates, of dreams, curses, oracles, the wrath of gods and grand themes such as may find in the Oresteia, of revenge pitted against lawful justice.

Here is an enjoyable game all serious readers can play, for many of us will have our own examples of such human moments in the literature of antiquity — an observation, an exchange, an emotional truth that leap across the years and give us proof of an innate and enduring human nature transcending historical, technological circumstances.

This is my own favourite — the first in a tryptych of dissent between the sexes that I'll present to you this evening.

Penelope has been waiting on Ithaca twenty years for the return of her beloved Odysseus. On the night of his return, she descends to the great hall and sees a figure sitting by the fire. But is it really him? (This is the Robert Fagels translation).

> One moment he seemed... Odysseus to the man, to the life —
> the next, no, he was not the man she knew,
> a huddled mass of rags was all she saw.

Then, the celebrated bed trick. She orders the wedding

bed to be moved from the bedroom. Only Odysseus, who constructed the bed himself, incorporating an ancient, deep-rooted olive tree, knows the bed is immoveable. And so he proves to Penelope's satisfaction that he's the man he says he is. But now he's upset at not being recognised. Contrite, she flings her arms around his neck.

> Odysseus — don't flare up at me now,
> not you, always the most understanding man alive!
> ... [don't be] angry with me now because I failed,
> at the first glimpse, to greet you, hold you, so...
> In my heart of hearts I always cringed with fear
> some fraud might come, beguile me with his talk.

They make their peace, of course. But we have witnessed close up, almost from the inside, the dynamics of a marital spat, a little hinge of misunderstanding and distress, and then its resolution. This is hardly a profound portrait of a self, but it yields a hint of one. Across a chasm of 2700 years this passage conveys the life of the emotions, a subjective reality, that we can intuitively understand.

Such points of light, moments of subjective revelation, are scattered right across the pre-modern centuries. Don't let any theorist tell you there were no selves before the 18th century. Apart from in Homer, we glimpse them in Plato, Marcus Aurelius, Virgil, in Catullus, Lucretius and Dante. We find a hint of a lively self in the 7th C Pillow Book of Sei Shonagon when the narrator, feeling a particular form of literary insult, observes, "There are also those times when you send someone a poem you're rather pleased with and fail to receive one in reply." We get a rich taste of subjective life in Chaucer and Petrarch, and countless poets. But these are moments, exceptional two or three lines that bring the inner life to the fore. The self was clearly there, but not yet considered to be a suitable subject for extended exploration, not yet a suitable subject for literature. One could imagine a simplified history of literature as the story of a steady expansion of acceptable subject matter.

We must wait until the early modern era to find a sustained investigation of that self. Just as in the month of May one might look across a meadow of unopened ox-eyed daisies pushing up, and notice that one has flowered fully before all the rest, so in cultural history, certain individuals explosively break through long before the others.

Which brings me to Michel de Montaigne.

He was active in the mid to late sixteenth century and surely was among the first to take himself as a serious subject, one for which he had to invent the appropriate literary form of the open-ended, discursive essay. His project was entirely self-conscious. He knew what he wanted. His contemporaries may have thought him indulgent when he declared, 'I am myself the matter of my book.' The modern reader is more immediately sympathetic. 'The world always looks straight ahead. As for me, I turn my gaze inwards, I fix it there and keep it busy... I have no business but with myself; I continually observe myself, I take stock of myself, I taste myself... I roll about in myself.'

To read the Essays is to witness one man single-handedly devising one of the essential conditions of modernity. In his Essay 'On Books' he claims the right to talk of matters that lie beyond his competence. In doing so, he'll reveal more about himself than about the matter in hand. 'And so the opinion I give [of books] is to declare the measure of my sight, not the measure of things.' And what is this self that emerges? Generous, tolerant, open-minded, suspicious of theory (rather odd in a Frenchman) and sceptical about the medical profession, about authorities in general, about theology and religious enthusiasm, ecstasies and visions. He's squeamish about violence, and is ahead of his time in disliking racism. He's an empiricist, loves friendship, has a relaxed will, takes an easy pleasure in life and human variety. He prefers the natural order of things. 'We are patchwork,' he says, 'The greatest thing in the world is to know how to belong to oneself.'

The Essays are among the brightest markers in the history of self-portrayal. Montaigne achieved a new way of seeing, of seeing oneself, and though the penny dropped slowly, after him there was no going back.

We might wonder if those essays were read in the original.

They may have made an impression on my other early flowering plant, Shakespeare. If one was writing a full-length history of the expression in literature of the subjective life, then one long chapter would have to be dedicated to the awesome mystery of Hamlet who, among all the fictive selves ever devised, leaps out of the darkness, the most fully conceived, cleverest, contrary, impenetrable, wholly real, entirely specific character ever devised. There are shades of Montaigne, even direct echoes, when Hamlet famously says — in prose — in Act 2 scene 2, "I have of late (but wherefore I know not) lost all my mirth, foregone all custom of exercise..." Here, a man is describing himself as depressed and says he doesn't know why. Even accounting for his dissembling before Rosencrantz and Guildenstern, in that 'but wherefore I know not' one senses the old dispensation of Aristotle and Galen and their unfounded certainties, their frail lines of untested knowledge begin to melt away before a new and typically modern form of self-doubt.

In some significant part, Hamlet must represent a self-portrait, for there can be no other way to construct so complex a consciousness without gazing hard into the mirror of selfhood.

There is no imaginary self before 1600 that can compare with this luminescent, transcendent mind. Even as late as the 1580s, playwrights other than Shakespeare were creating characters that were still dominated by a single vice or virtue.

The dominating figure of Hamlet stands at the beginning of a long tradition of complex, multi-faceted characters whom we can never completely define. Just as with real people, we can disagree about them. This degree of impenetrability seems to ensure their survival through the years. Elizabeth Bennet, Madame Bovary, Anna Karenina, Stephen Dedalus — we all have our lists.

* * *

I have been making no distinction here between the self-portrait and the portrait of a self. That is, between a self-portrayal by an existing or historically real individual, and an invented, fictional self dreamed up by a story-teller, like a character in a novel or a play. Both the self-portrait and fictional portrait present us with a continuous, privately experienced entity of the kind I've discussed; a unique ghostly person; a centre of awareness and identity, the 'me' that experiences pain, feels emotion, has memories, discernment, agency. Some authorities make the case that such selfhood is largely an invention, a cultural product, bound by time and historical circumstance. One of the most eloquent expressions of this view will be found in Jacob Burkhardt's The Civilisation of the Renaissance in Italy and this justly celebrated passage. He refers first to the medieval mind — "... both sides of human consciousness — the side turned to the world and that turned inward — lay, as it were, beneath a common veil, dreaming or half awake. The veil was woven of faith, childlike prejudices, and illusion; man recognised himself only as a member of a race, a nation, a party, a corporation, a family or in some other general category. It was in Italy that this veil first melted into thin air, and awakened an objective perception and treatment of the state and all things of this world in general; but by its side, and with full power, there also arose the subjective; man becomes a self-aware individual and recognises himself as such... At the close of the C13, Italy began to swarm with individuality; the ban laid upon human personality was dissolved."

Opposed to this view of self-hood as an artefact of culture is the idea the self was always there in some degree, in precisely the terms that Locke describes — the self as the inevitable biological product, like consciousness itself, of a certain volume of pre-frontal neural capacity. Even a dog is the recipient of its own pain, its own joy. It is more probable that human self-awareness has always lain along a spectrum; cultures, and especially their arts, play the crucial role in cumulatively, incrementally, moving us along that spectrum. History shows us that there are also circumstances that can move us back the other way. War and famine come to mind. Nothing narrows the mind like fear or hunger. There have always been selves — but the point remains: it is culture that grants the conditions in which the self becomes a subject in our literature.

The fully-realised self-portrait, or the portrait of an imaginary self do not show us an idealised form, or a type or a moral example to which we must aspire, or in imitation of which we might hope to enter heaven, but an individual representing nothing other than him or herself. And therefore, as all humans must be, as flawed as he or she is virtuous. Necessarily, the writer who delves must also be capable of a feat of detachment, even of scepticism. The language of such a portrayal must perform the difficult task of plausibly conveying an inner state and, at best, show change through time and circumstance, through shifting emotions. We effortlessly inhabit the so-called qualia of our quotidian lives but cannot easily project them onto the page. For that to happen, the appropriate literary means must be invented; reciprocally, self-expression has driven the development of the forms. The heroic saga will not do. What will? The intimate letter, the journal, the memoir, the confession, even the ship's log, and ultimately the novel.

But that's enough for now of what Nabokov once called 'the moonshine of generalisation'. Here's a second marital row. It is January 9 1663, Samuel Pepys is lying in bed one morning rather late — unusual for him. He often goes to his nearby office as early as 4 am. But the night before he has been to the theatre with his wife, Elizabeth and afterwards they had to wait almost an hour for a cab home. He wakes to find his wife standing before him in great distress. Two months before she wrote him a letter expressing her unhappiness in the marriage. In particular, she has felt lonely and excluded. But Pepys burned the letter without even reading it. Elizabeth has a copy and 'She now read it, and it was so piquant, and wrote in English, and most of it true, of the retiredness of her life and how unpleasant it was.'

Pepys's immediate concern is of her letter falling into someone's hands — 'so much disgrace to me and dishonour, if it should have been found by anybody.' He goes on —

> 'I was vexed at it, and desired her and then commanded her to tear it. When she desired to be excused it, I forced it from her, and tore it, and withal took her bundle of papers from her, and leapt out of the bed and in my shirt clapped them into the pocket of my breeches, that she might not get them from me, and having got on my stockings and breeches and gown, I pulled them out one by one and tore them all before her face, though it went against my heart to do it, she crying and desiring me not to do it, but such was my passion and trouble to see the letters of my love to her...'

Claire Tomalin highlights this scene in her superb biography of Pepys. One of the epigraphs she has chosen is the judgement of Robert Louis Stevenson, which speaks of 'that unflinching — I almost said that unintelligent — sincerity which makes it a miracle among human books. Whether he did ill or well he was still his own unequalled self.'

'The unequalled self' is the apt subtitle of Tomalin's book. In this scene, a turning point in the marriage, Pepys forensically lays out his own anger, his cruelty, his hollow concern for his reputation, his violence, and then his remorse ('and the truth is I am sorry for the tearing of so many poor loving letters of mine from sea and elsewhere to her'); and as well, a full understanding of Elizabeth's misery, pity for her and an acceptance of the justness of her complaints. Not even his friend and fellow diarist, John Evelyn, touched on domestic matters like this.

Again, here is a case of literature expanding by subject matter. Pepys truly was the unequalled self. His maturity, his range, his connections through the highest levels of politics and society, his awareness of contemporary events, situate him beautifully not only as the chronicler of his age but also of the intimate man, endowed with the gift of clinical self-detachment. Pepys might almost be considered a kind of scientist of the self. He was writing at the time of the establishment of the Royal Society (he was a Fellow from 1665 and had many scientist friends). His milieu was not only the Restoration but the English Enlightenment, during a heady time when most of the world's science was concentrated in a triangle formed by Oxford, Cambridge and

London. Objectivity was a term coming into use. It could be turned on the self.

* * *

We go forwards a hundred years to locate our third account of a man and woman in disagreement, this time in embarrassing circumstances. The year is 1763. A young man, James Boswell, barely 22 years old and, by his own admission, very much on the make in London, wakes to the experience of a burning sensation in the most tender part of his manhood. He has gonorrhoea, and he blames his lover, Louisa, an actress, for giving it to him. He bitterly reflects all morning. 'Am I, who have had safe and elegant intrigues with fine women become the dupe of a strumpet? Am I now to be laid up for many weeks to suffer extreme pain and full confinement... must I have my poor pocket drained... And then, am I prevented from making love to Lady Mirabel, or any other woman of fashion?.' And yet he has boasted to this same Lady Mirabel only recently that he 'runs up and down this town just like a wild colt.' His Louisa who, on their first encounter, by Boswell's exquisite account, coaxed him sweetly through a session of impotence brought on by depression, has told Boswell that she cannot imagine life without him.

He confronts Louisa in precisely the manner he has prepared and formulated in his journal — cold and polite.

The conversation is set out in the form of a play. (Louisa: My dear Sir! I hope you are well today. Boswell: Excessively well, I thank you.) Eventually, he comes to the point. Horrified, she tells him that she's been with no other man but him for 6 months. She had a bout of the disease but has been clear for 15 months. He ends the meeting, rising from his chair with the words, 'Madam, your most obedient servant.'

At home, he confides to his journal: 'During all this conversation, I really behaved with a manly composure and polite dignity that could not fail to inspire awe... thus ended my intrigue with the fair Louisa, which I flattered myself so much with, and from which I expected at least a winter's safe copulation. It is indeed very hard.'

A while later he writes an angry, rather vicious letter demanding money from her to meet his surgeon's bill. 'Yet I thought to mention the money was not so genteel. However, if I get it, (which is not probable), it will be of real service to me.' She does indeed send it. Finally, Boswell consoles himself that 'Louisa was only in the mean time, till I got into genteel life... a woman of fashion was the only proper object for such a man as me.'

It is a highly revealing and damning portrait by an ambitious young man. He is using all his meagre contacts to get a commission in the Army. But he doesn't want to be a soldier; he wants to cut a figure around London as a gentleman and a man of fashion. He therefore wants a regiment (the Guards) that is unlikely to be sent abroad. He hates the idea of sleeping in a tent, and of an uncomfortable bed. What's remarkable about Boswell's Journals at their best is their highly developed concept of a self, — not noble, heroic, admirable, but flawed and venal. The paradox is the distance he can measure out in his self-portrayal to show us a man deceiving himself.

We are the fortunate beneficiaries of a decision James Boswell took in 1762 to write "the history of my mind" . He shows himself variously as witty, charming in company, well-read for his age, kind to beggars, and also indolent, self-pitying, ruthless when it suits him, a preening hypocrite, a pompous toady, a depressive, sometimes cruel, sometimes untruthful man on the make, acutely conscious of status and rank, and desperate for the estate of a gentleman. He writes well, his memory is prodigious, his eye for detail, for the flow of conversation is exquisite, as is his self-detachment. He's prepared, and at such a tender age, to show us every side of his personality. He gives us a self.

By the time he was writing, Boswell had precedents, but not many. By the mid 18th century, the novel, which as a literary form was a vector for the growth of the idea of the self, was beginning to be well-established. Jane Austen was only a long generation away, and a generation beyond her waits Flaubert.

* * *

The novel as it developed in the eighteenth century and as its readership grew, seems, at its very inception, to arrive with a firm understanding of the representation of the subjective. Samuel Richardson's Clarissa, published in 1748, nearly a million words long, has been described by some as the first extended representation of consciousness in the history of literature. Would it have been possible without Montaigne and Shakespeare? Almost certainly, for many other factors were in play in the rise of the novel. Still, one of the greatest critics and expositors of Shakespeare who ever lived, Samuel Johnson, praised Clarissa as "the first book in the world for the knowledge it displays of the human heart."

In its early maturity the English novel delighted in seeming 'real' — the true account, the discovered letters, the memoir of a shipwrecked traveller surviving alone on a desert island, the device of 'in the year 176-, in the town of L-.' Then soon, it was mocking and subverting its grip on the real in the manic comedy of Tristram Shandy. But there was yet another enabling device that made the act of reading a novel analogous to thought itself. This was a means of blurring the distinction between an objective description and a subjective feeling. A third person account could, whenever it suited the writer, be coloured by the feelings of a character. And such a character could become the focal point of consciousness, without having to be locked into a first person. The term 'free indirect style' was invented to describe the fictional techniques of Flaubert, but it arrives fully formed in the work of Jane Austen. Since then it's been firmly embedded in the art of the novel, and is barely noticed by the common reader. The self is diffused through the physical or social landscape of the novel.

I've omitted so far any mention of religion. Briefly, two considerations. First, there is a widely held view that nothing promoted the awareness of self than communion with a divine being. And second, the development of the novel and its subjective preoccupations owed much to Protestantism.

There must be substance to both, if only because so many serious thinkers have made those points. I retain just a little scepticism. Before Montaigne, Christianity had more than fifteen centuries to foster a sense of heightened individuality. The results were poor and were surely intended to be so. In the written Christian tradition of meditations on the godhead, the sincere intent was not to elevate selfhood but to dissolve it before a higher presence. Humility demandsedit. When one is awed in the presence of an omnipotent being, it is difficult or, rather, unnecessary, to contemplate the self. Reading in St. Augustine's Confessions or in The Revelations of Divine Love by Julian of Norwich, one has the impression that the preoccupation with sin and the necessity of conversion of others bury the self. Self-abnegation, self-denial — the point is surely to move away from considerations of personal identity.

The religious poetry of George Herbert, among the

greatest in the English canon, doesn't lead us towards a self, any more than Milton's Paradise Lost does. We know far less about the narrator of Herbert's poems than we do about Montaigne, Anna Karenina, Pepys or Boswell. And that was never the point. Herbert's poems are more like prayers, piety braided with consummate cleverness and supreme poetic artistry.

There was an opportunity which, if taken, might have radically transformed the path of the western intellectual tradition. As Flaubert famously wrote to Madame Roger de Genettes, 'With the gods gone and Christ yet to come, there was a unique moment, from Cicero to Marcus Aurelius, when man stood alone. Nowhere else do I find that particular grandeur...'

He had Lucretius in mind when he wrote that. Early Christianity was murderously intolerant of the kind of free enquiry represented by Lucretius, who was active in the first century before Christ. His universe contained no consoling God, no purpose, no immortality, no meaning beyond that which humans could bestow. His tradition, derived from a line of descent from Democritus and Epicurus, lay buried from general view for centuries. Christianity, with its emphasis on suffering and sacrifice rather than well-being for oneself and others, for incurious faith rather than sceptical investigation, was, from the Lucretian perspective, a numbing diversion. Its grip began to loosen in the seventeenth century even as it was in a frenzy of killing over theological differences during the Thirty Years War. ("Only religion" , Lucretius wrote in De Rerum Natura of another conflict, "Could produce such evil.")

The slow evolution of trade and specialisation, so well described by Adam Smith, allowed the burden of constant labour to be lifted from the backs of mankind and granted the luxury of solitude, at least to a privileged few. It's a matter of celebration that their numbers — our numbers — have swollen over the centuries. Only in the luxury of solitude can one indulge the discovery of self in what Flaubert called in that same letter, referring to Lucretius, 'the fixity of a pensive gaze'. But there can be no such solitude, indeed, ultimately no privacy, in the presence of a jealous God. This is not to argue, of course, that believers have less of a self than anyone else — rather, that the literary tradition of religious contemplation and published sermons of the kind so popular in the 17th and 18 centuries, challenged the emergence of a flourishing self represented by Pepys and Boswell — both men, it should be conceded, of minimal humility.

As for Protestantism — the novel's essential pluralism, its blithe freedoms and sympathies and the aesthetic difficulty of incorporating a deus ex machina into plausible narratives, make it above all a secular form. Graham Greene, for example, is at his weakest (some would say, most absurd) when he allows God to take control of his plot, as in The End of the Affair.

Montaigne was happy to live an epicurean life within the shelter of his Catholicism. He loathed theological enquiry. One searches hard through the three dozen plays of Shakespeare to find an explicit and sustained endorsement of specifically Christian dogma — and not much of a mention of Jesus, or even Mary. Pepys and Boswell lived within a conventional form of Anglicanism, but its tenets barely intruded on their thoughts and certainly not on their behaviour. These, my early blossoming oxeyed daisies, were in essence secular spirits. All four, I would say, were adepts of the good life. Only the pre-Christian or the modern era could have contained them.

We are now largely godless in the intellectual fortresses of the West, and whether we like it or not, we've come to be, largely through varieties of philosophical materialism, the inheritors of the tradition of Democritus, Epicurus and Lucretius. Even those who care nothing for science, have absorbed more of its world view than they might care to admit. I would say that the seventeenth and early eighteenth centuries, when science and philosophy were one, was our great and slow turning point.

Since then, self-awareness has spread but not necessarily grown. We have not made so much progress in the business of 'knowing thyself'. We may be self-aware collectively, but what remains is our helplessness before the events we collectively inspire. This, despite all our technologies and our ebbing superstitions. However, our literature, to return to Bob Dylan, continues to be the process by which we give ourselves a good talking to.

Even as we identify the brain with the mind, we remain astonished that a self could arise from mere stuff and portray itself, that the self is not the cause of thought but its product. In the European West, at least, many of us have returned to that space that Flaubert identified — after the death of the Roman gods and before the coming of Christ. We are both bereft of a consoling deity and relieved of his commands. Our times are harder but more interesting. We may gather en masse at tourist sites like the Parthenon, smart phones in hand, and take 'selfies'; within the contemporary movement of identity politics and sexual preference, we should rise to the common courtesy of letting people be who and how they want to be — but we are, all of us, ultimately alone with the matter of the self, of our selves as we confront, as did Hamlet, this 'quintessence of dust'.

Ian McEwan
Science
Copyright © by Ian McEwan 2019
This edition arranged with ROGERS, COLERIDGE & WHITE LTD. (RCW)
Through Big Apple Agency, Inc., Labuan, Malaysia.
Simplified Chinese edition copyright:
2022 Shanghai Translation Publishing House (STPH)
All rights reserved.

图字：09-2020-825号

图书在版编目(CIP)数据

当我们谈论科学时,我们在谈论什么/(英)伊恩·麦克尤恩(Ian McEwan)著;孙灿译.—上海：上海译文出版社,2021.12
(麦克尤恩双语作品)
书名原文：Science
ISBN 978-7-5327-8712-8

Ⅰ.①当… Ⅱ.①伊…②孙… Ⅲ.①随笔—作品集—英国—现代 Ⅳ.①I561.65

中国版本图书馆CIP数据核字(2021)第232404号

当我们谈论科学时，我们在谈论什么(Science)
〔英〕伊恩·麦克尤恩 著 孙 灿 译
责任编辑/宋玲 装帧设计/张志全工作室

上海译文出版社有限公司出版、发行
网址：www.yiwen.com.cn
201101 上海市闵行区号景路159弄B座
上海雅昌艺术印刷有限公司印刷

开本787×1092 1/32 印张8.25 插页6 字数60,000
2022年3月第1版 2022年3月第1次印刷
印数：0,001-6,000册

ISBN 978-7-5327-8712-8/I·5378
定价：69.00元

本书版权为本社独家所有，非经本社同意不得转载、摘编或复制
本书如有质量问题，请与承印厂质量科联系. T: 021-68798999